With a Cast of the Dice

By Magnus October

Edited by @rayfinnwrites
Cover art by @tomomochi

Chapter 1

Fen

The sounds of the ballroom echoed down every hallway of the castle, gracing Fen's ears with a calm that he so desperately needed. It had been many moons since the last ball he attended. This was the first he took at its value; the others before were merely waves of events crashing over him until the storm of it subsided. After it all, he had found himself in bed, hardly remembering all he endured. He did not hate balls so much as feared them, his nerves on all ends sparking in his body as he danced, drank, and conversed. It was a duty, he understood this, one he could handle despite the frazzled aftermath of it all. At the very least, he loved dressing the part.

Though his stomach clenched in anxiety, Fen made his way to the grand hall, the music becoming louder with each step. The jingling of his necklaces and earrings became more muffled as the sound of strings and pianos gave way to a new feeling creeping into him. *What was this?* He tucked a loose strand of hair behind his ear, checking his polished black dress shoes for any signs of scuffs or untied laces. No such imperfections showed themselves, and he supposed he was as ready as he ever would be. With a deep breath, he exhaled all of his last solitary moments—for the next few hours at the very least— and pushed open the ornate wooden door to enter the source of the melody.

No one turned their head at the door's rather loud opening squeak; the music was loud enough to divert attention. Everyone was already enjoying themselves or, at least, had the air of enjoyment aiding their facade. Fen wondered if he too could put on a show of ease, deciding he would at least try. He looked around, trying to scope out any familiar faces in the ocean of well-dressed vampires. After a moment of adjusting to the new environment, he took several cautious glances, steeled his resolve, and marched on.

Every corner of the ballroom was immaculate, though not all to Fen's taste. He may have lived in the same castle, but he was not responsible for the decor, to be sure. Golden flowers were clearly the theme; they were crafted onto the pillars and spiraling up to the ceiling, with golden vines snaking onto the walls. The ceiling was so brightly lit with chandeliers that he could hardly recognize the paintings he knew were there, all soft brushstrokes and cherubs and too many biblical references for him. Tables lined the outer walls, crowded with crystalline dishware awash with a spread he could hardly wrap his head

4

around, though what caught his eye were the glasses all lined perfectly, ripe for the taking. He had to find something to occupy himself with, or this was going to be a very long party.

Stepping down marble stairs with intricately woven rugs spread before him, he took another quick glance around the room. His height was a hindrance in that moment, as he could only make out so many people in the chaos of dancing and socializing. *There are too many people here*, he thought, *and they whisper so much it makes me... nervous.* His thoughts became more comfortable once he had a cup in hand, looking down into a deep red liquid he had made peace with long ago. Taking his first sip, he decided to make his way around the perimeter, trying his best to look as if he wasn't a little lost. He hoped he did not look as nervous as he felt, and yet his stomach held that same strange knot whose origin he couldn't quite place.

What is this feeling?

A lively tune began, violinists working their expert bows along strings, goading on the air of revelry that had Fen smiling, albeit only slightly. Though these balls had many vampires trouncing into his home, whispering and glancing in ways he did not like, he at least enjoyed the music. He hoped he could find a dance partner this time, one that did not make him feel like a ripe grape upon a vine. At previous balls, he either did not dance at all or found his partner to be anything but what he envisioned. Though he sighed thinking about it, he wondered if his standards were simply too high.

After circling the ballroom once, the time flying by faster than he anticipated, Fen realized he had to pick a spot to plant his feet before making a fool of himself by walking the outside of the room like a restless dog. Taking another sip of his drink, he felt just the slightest bit brave. That biting feeling in his stomach reared again, his annoyance growing. He did not like not knowing things, especially his own feelings. *Why do I feel like… maybe something is going to happen?* He paused. *Or is this more like… excitement?*

As he came to his awaited conclusion, a familiar voice grabbed his attention. Turning around, he finally found a face he recognized and even welcomed.

"Lorcan, thank God you found me," he said. "I was starting to think I was going to have to spend the whole ball in silence."

Lorcan grinned, their blue eyes crinkling at the sides, freckled cheeks growing. They beckoned to Fen with a hand, urging him to come closer.

He obliged, taking a few steps towards Lorcan to close the space between them. His friend looked around a moment, then leaned down to whisper mischievously.

"So… is your plan still on?"

A blush formed on Fen's cheeks and ears, his face growing warm. "I mean, as long as I don't lose my nerve, but you said you wouldn't tease me about it!"

Lorcan smiled again, a mischief clouding their face that was all too familiar to Fen. "I didn't mean to tease you. I meant to remind you, and make sure you don't chicken out."

He rolled his eyes at his friend, taking in their outfit for the first time.

Lorcan was, if nothing else, confident in social settings. Their suit practically screamed it, floral patterned from head to toe in all manner of colors, with a white satin bow tie and short auburn hair styled upwards. They always looked put-together, even in more casual settings, but balls were an event they always looked forward to. Fen knew they loved the intrigue of it all; the scheming and cunning were something they, like all other vampires, thrived in. Lorcan loved secrets, and more so loved making people pay for them.

Fen, despite having Lorcan as a best friend, could not understand those feelings. What was so great about being dishonest? Why was it vampire culture to be devious? He couldn't bring himself to be that way even if he wanted to. He wished, not for the first time in his second life, that he had more of an understanding of the vampire culture he occupied. He also hoped this ball might be the first step in doing so—if fate allowed.

"Honestly, Lorcan, it might be good if you *were* to peer pressure me tonight. I already felt so nervous walking in."

"You always are in these things; I know the tone isn't really for you, but you look too damn good not to do something different this time!"

Fen smiled genuinely at his friend. Even if they loved secrets, he knew they wouldn't lie, not to him. It was also comforting to have some reassurance that his clothing wasn't too much. Casually, he tried to stay in more modern attire, but for balls, he wanted nothing more than to look the part of what he was. Suits and form-fitting dresses were most popular, with some feminine vampires going all out in ballgowns, which he appreciated. Fen loved the more classically cliche vampire attire: tight black pants, elegant black shoes, and layered blouses that might as well be labeled as costumes. If it wasn't for his many silver necklaces, earrings, rings, and an upper-middle lip piercing, he could pass for a much older vampire who stepped

8

out of time. His constant black-painted nails and eyeliner finished off the look and made him thankful that even if this ball did not go as he wanted, at least he looked good.

"Thanks, you don't look too bad yourself," Fen replied.

"Thank you, kind Prince," Lorcan teased. "If all else fails tonight, I'll dance with you if you have your heart set on it."

He shook his head. "I love you, but I'm not interested in a pity dance for your single friend."

They winked at Fen. "It might be a pity dance, but at least I dance better than a lot of the guys you choose."

"I hardly choose them myself," sighed Fen. "Queen Eluvia somehow sends them to me, and while I appreciate her trying, they're always so…"

"I know, they're probably a little too crafty for you," Lorcan interrupted.

"That's one way to put it, yeah."

"But this time, you'll be the one trying. You're going to put yourself out there, and you're going to find someone, I feel it." Lorcan paused. "Or, at least find someone hot."

Fen laughed softly, appreciating in that moment just how much Lorcan eased his mind. He still had the ache of excitement in his stomach, but he had to admit he felt more ready. If worst comes to worst, there's always another ball. The chances of finding another vampire whose main hobby wasn't being serpentine seemed impossible, but at least he would try tonight.

The upbeat song ended, many attendees clapping and the musicians taking quick bows before moving on to the next. Fen looked at Lorcan, trying to exchange a look. Lorcan thankfully nodded back in understanding, and they split up. Fen started another ring around the ballroom to his right side, and Lorcan did the same on the left. They would meet back up again eventually, presenting any potential dance partners to each other. It was a silly, childish plan, and Fen silently thanked Lorcan for going along with it.

As he walked and scanned the crowd, another batch of guests entered the room, thunderous laughs blending into the noise already established. Fen focused his eyes there, the new sounds drawing his attention, until something else vied for all of it.

Among the group, one man in a simple black tuxedo ensemble made Fen's breath catch. The man wore all black: pants, shoes, blazer, undershirt, and a full-length satin tie. His deep brown hair was hardly styled with purpose, yet it somehow looked just as it should, a single streak of red among the rest. His hair was parted down the middle and a texture only described in Fen's mind as fluffy, though not frizzy at all. He was tall and well-built with a frame that seemed to have just the right amount of muscle. His features were sharp, all angles and a frustratingly handsome jaw. When looking closer, Fen noticed his pale hands were heavily tattooed, and what looked to be a design of thorny vines was tattooed on his neck, the ink peeking out of his collar.

The man walked in alone, speaking to no one at all, making his way to the drink table with a certainty Fen could only imagine himself having. He seemed so sure, swiping a glass from the table, taking a long swig, and carefully holding it in his hand, the other in his pants pocket. Fen realized he had been watching for what was most likely a little too long, and hoped that no one noticed in the frenzy of greetings and pleasantries. He had to talk to this man, sensing immediately that he was a newcomer. His aura was so inherently *different*. The man was there with a purpose that was anyone's guess, and Fen was determined to find out. He felt seemingly possessed by a bravery he did not know he had. Maybe it was the curiosity that cats were rumored to fall to, but he did not care. This felt like the best chance he was going to get tonight, and he could not let it slip away.

Chapter 2

Soren

Adjusting his earpiece of impressively minuscule size, Soren followed a group of vampires that he would rather have never interacted with, into a castle he would never enter, and into a ball he would never, ever have gone to. It was an entire setting of spectacle, full of Royals all on their best nasty behavior. He could not wipe the sour look plastered onto his face, using all his self-control not to rip off the earpiece and storm back out into the night, never to set foot in this place again. Well, unless it was for a more worthwhile purpose, and this was not his idea of worthwhile. His suit, though fitted well, felt unlike him and his usual more leather-clad wardrobe. At least he had been allowed to pick the color.

Even amongst the small group he inserted himself into, he felt isolated and wrong. These were not his people, nor would he ever want them to be. His nails dug into his palms, a heat gathering there against his better judgment, but he did not let it get past that. He could not let his hatred rule him tonight; there was a time and place for it. He entered a blinding room of opulent gold and crystal, music flowing into his ears like a thread in the eye of a needle, conversation and laughter booming onto the stage of his senses. This he could manage; it was the talking he worried about.

He followed along down the stairs onto the main floor, catching sight of a table full of glasses topped off with blood. If he could not enjoy himself at the ball, the Rogues could at least let him partake in the free refreshments. Against his logic and knowledge of himself, they'd still assigned him this mission. They sent him under the guise of being able to take care of himself, should things go south. He didn't think they knew just how many vampires would be attending the ball, how labyrinthine the castle would be once inside, or how heated Soren would get upon entering his own personal den of wolves. And wolves they all were, stalking prey and forming packs, peripherals always alert, waiting for a chance to strike. It was maddening, watching them all in such a state of revelry while he wanted nothing more than to get in and get out without causing a scene.

Soren sighed deeply, strengthening his resolve as his feet carried him to the table of blood, grabbing one perhaps a tad too harshly, and taking one long drink before holding it in his hand as casually as he could. He set his sights on the crowd, awaiting instruction.

It came, a soft voice sounding through the earpiece in a whisper.

"Soren? Can you hear me?"

"Yeah, you could stand to be a little louder, though, you didn't tell me how noisy a ball would be," replied Soren, trying his best to be subtle while seemingly speaking to himself.

"I'll try my best. I have eyes on you, but I have my own things to take care of, so I won't be on you 24/7. I've scoped out as many Royals as I could for you. You just walk; I'll tell you when."

"Got it."

Soren followed orders, going to take a step to his left and walk around the tables until his contact told him who to speak with and when. The other Rogues wanted information, and he was going to make damn sure he got as much as he could as quickly as possible so he would be free to leave. Then, he could get back to them and plan the next steps. That is, if he could manage to get anything useful. As his foot landed on the ground in his first step away, he heard someone clearing their throat to his right, directly next to him. To say he wasn't a bit startled

14

would be a lie, but at least he'd avoided jumping. He turned his body to face the source.

Standing tensely next to him was a man. The vampire was shorter than Soren, adorned with all silver jewelry and the most vampiric clothes he could picture, with almost shoulder-length black hair, slightly waved enough to give it texture. He had Chinese features, and when he made eye contact, he could see just a small amount of red on his cheeks. What caught him off guard the most were his eyes. This man had eyes like a forest, deep and green, with a look of determination mixed with embarrassment. He seemed shy, something no other vampire in the room had the tact to be, and it made Soren feel as if he had to leave then and there. He looked at the man a moment longer, his stance paralyzed there in front of him, like a lamb led to slaughter.

Soren's chest tightened in anticipation before the man spoke, and it struck him as his lips parted that Soren thought he was beautiful. Objectively, of course.

"Hi," he said, outstretching a hand of black nails and silver rings. "I am Prince Fen. I… I hope you're enjoying the refreshments so far."

Soren could not determine what this "Prince Fen's" purpose was. Royals always had a purpose: they did nothing that would not gain them something or bring them pleasure. He knew this as fact. All of them were entangled in their own games: Kings, Queens, Monarchs, and the leaders of Royal houses, all rich and powerful and ruthless. The Princes, Princesses, and Majesties were no different in personality, their Royal leaders sponsoring whatever their hearts desired. The Delegation—the group of older vampires that governed them—were no better, perhaps even worse in Soren's mind. They were easily bought; laws and regulations swayed at the drop of a coin, of which the Royals had no shortage.

Where did that leave the rest—the vampires unclaimed by Royals, or the ones that realized the hell for what it was and left? The Rogues were a category of vampires who, at best, wanted to lead simple lives and, at worst (according to the Royals), wanted to destroy and rebuild. Soren did not fault the Rogues living amongst humans or themselves; he could empathize with the desire to simply be, and do nothing more. He, however, would not sit idly by while the Royals still had all the control. He would aid the Rogue group in tearing down all they had, and build anew. He had to.

Soren blinked, realizing he had waited a beat too long in replying to Prince Fen. He knew he would have to lie and say he was a Royal as well. The thought was bitter as it sat on his tongue, waiting to be spoken into existence. Just before he did, he felt a strange guilt looking into Prince Fen's eyes.

"Prince So–" he stopped himself. Giving out his true name in this place would not be his wisest move. What was it about this Prince that made him want to speak the truth?

He cleared his throat, attempting to cover up his stumble. "Prince Sona, pleased to meet you." Soren shook the other vampire's hand, a tad proud of himself for coming up with a name on the spot.

Prince Fen beamed up at him, and it was endearing, despite Soren not wanting it to be.

When they both withdrew their hands, Soren realized he hadn't answered his other comment.

I need to get it together, he thought. *I can't get information like this.*

"Oh! Sorry, yes, the blood is very good here. The glasses are… also nice."

Shit.

Prince Fen kept a soft smile on his lips, nodding. "I'm glad you think so." For a brief moment that he almost didn't see, Soren watched as his smile turned into a frown and he bit his lip, though his composure returned quickly.

17

A moment of awkward silence spread between them, Soren not knowing how to respond and Prince Fen fidgeting in place. The Prince's body swayed from side to side, feet unable to stay still. Soren wondered if he should say something, though he didn't know where to begin. This man was beginning to make him annoyed at himself, breaking the persona he so desperately needed that night. He took a sip from his cup, and Prince Fen followed suit. That made Soren crack a smile.

Prince Fen returned it—a genuine one. "I'm sorry, I don't tend to do this often."

Soren could work with this. "Do what? Come to balls, or approach strangers?"

"The second. I have to come to these things a lot. I like to leave early though—too many people."

Soren nodded in understanding and decided to press a bit. "Why do it now then?"

Prince Fen's eyes widened, cheeks growing red again along with the tips of his ears. Again, it was endearing, and Soren hated that.

"I… I'll be honest, it's stupid. Can we talk about something else?"

Soren did not frown, though he wanted to. Now he was curious, but it could wait as Prince Fen spoke up again.

18

"How about this: I ask you something, and if you answer it, I'll answer your question?"

Soren's stomach dropped, only a bit. What kind of question? Was he found out somehow? His contact hadn't said anything; what if they were taken out?

Better to be casual.

"Sure, depends on the question though."

Prince Fen looked away sheepishly and, without looking back, said, "I know a lot of Royals, and I know what they're all like. I got this... this gut feeling when I saw you that you're either new or..." he trailed off, shaking his head quickly before finishing. "Or maybe you just don't go out much?"

Soren almost sighed in relief. His cover could easily be that he was a new vampire, just adopted into a Royal house, and then this Prince could make it believable. Fen could ease any suspicions, vouching for this "new Royal" at the ball. He could use that, but the pang of guilt from before returned, and he silently cursed at himself. Why would he feel so guilty lying to a Prince? Why did he feel the need to be honest with him, against all his better judgment?

He looked at Prince Fen's anxious face, noticing how pretty his features were, the word coming to mind being *soft*.

That had to be the reason—nothing more. He was attractive, and that was all. He could get past that—easily.

As he was about to answer, the voice in the earpiece came back with a tone he did not think he deserved.

"*What are you doing?*" they asked.

Soren smiled apologetically. "I am so sorry, could you actually just give me a moment? The music is very loud and I need to get away from it; I'll be right back."

Prince Fen looked stricken but recomposed himself. "Yes, I'll wait here. Take your time."

As quickly as he could without drawing attention, Soren went back up the steps and through a side door, not knowing where it led. He did not care, however, as long as it was away from Prince Fen and allowed him a chance to clear his head.

Once he shut the door behind him, he looked around, surveying. No one was there—good.

The voice in the earpiece came again before Soren could respond. "Okay, now you up and ditch? What were you doing?"

"I was doing my job," Soren replied, annoyed. "I was trying to get information. I was pretty sure you knew that."

He could practically hear them gritting their teeth. "I told you, I had people in mind. *He* was not one of them. You need to

20

find a way to ignore him or get him to leave you alone so you can continue the mission."

Soren found this odd, to say the least. The other Rogues said no such thing about only speaking to certain vampires. His contact had only said they had some worthwhile marks in mind —nothing more. What was their aversion to him speaking with Prince Fen?

"Why? Shouldn't I talk to as many people as possible? The more information, the better. That's what they said. You're just the contact; you don't call all the shots."

"I do about this. Talk to anyone but him." They paused. "And also maybe Queen Eluvia; don't talk to her either."

Soren let his annoyed tone shine; he knew his mission and didn't like that his contact seemed to be keeping something from him. "Sure, I'll stay away from the Queen of the castle, but that Prince approached *me*, so as far as I'm concerned, he's a free ticket."

His contact said more, but Soren didn't listen. His resolve was set, and he would do his mission as instructed, not letting his bothersome contact get in his way. That was the only reason, and certainly not that he was intrigued by this Prince and his shocking sincerity.

Chapter 3

Fen

W*ell, things could be going worse, I suppose*, thought Fen. He had mustered enough courage to go and speak with the mystery vampire, and then Sona had just… run away. Had he said something wrong? Did he somehow poke a nerve? It was maddening as he stood there alone, waiting like a fool for him to come back. At least the Prince had said he *would* come back; that was something. Sona himself was also something. As Fen saw him up close and spoke to him, he felt embarrassed for being so flustered. Prince Sona was taller, had a vertical eyebrow piercing on each side in the middle of his brows with black jewelry, and when he had gone to lift his cup to drink, his sleeve had revealed more tattoos going past his hands and onto his arms. He was also so refreshingly *normal*. Well, normal by Fen's standards. All he wanted were vampires like him, who did not prioritize secrets and power, and it had seemed a daunting task.

Prince Sona was the closest he had seen besides Lorcan, though he knew Lorcan well enough to know they were still as cunning a vampire as they needed to be. As he waited, he finished his glass of blood and grabbed a second, if only to look occupied until Prince Sona returned. Thankfully, he did not have to wait long. After only one more drink, the door he was watching opened, and out came Sona.

Fen bristled, seeing the expression on his face, one of annoyance and resolution all at once. He walked with a purpose, right back to him. It made Fen's chest tighten, only a little.

Prince Sona stood before him again, running a hand through his hair and shrugging. "Sorry, just not used to these things yet."

Fen nodded, trying not to seem too happy. "I understand. It takes some getting used to, for sure."

"I believe you. I think I owe you an answer to your question too, don't I?"

"You don't have to. That is, unless you want me to answer yours." He said this more flirtatiously than he meant to, cringing at himself internally.

Prince Sona did not seem taken aback, and even returned the energy. "I'd like that. So, here's your answer: Yes, I am new, just turned recently and adopted into a Royal house. I was trying not to be too obvious about this being my first ball, but I guess you're seeing firsthand that I did a bad job."

"No, no, you're not doing a bad job!" Fen amended, maybe a bit too enthusiastically. "I mean, I think I'm the only one who noticed. Everyone else at these things already has a goal or two in mind, knows who they want to talk to, and they don't really pay attention to anyone else."

Prince Sona raised an eyebrow. "What kind of goals?"

Fen could feel his face grow hot and he tried his best to quell it. He hoped he didn't reveal his own reason for being there, otherwise, he may have passed away from embarrassment. "I guess most people think of the balls as either a business venture, a way to make connections, or a chance to reconnect—or perhaps even..." Did he truly have to say it? He was already too far into the sentence to backtrack. "A way of courting, I suppose?"

If Prince Sona sensed anything off with Fen, he did not show it. He simply nodded, taking a sip of blood. "That's good to know. Which are you here for?"

The heat in Fen's face heightened to a point he could no longer ignore, and he failed to keep his expression in check. He thought about excusing himself and never returning, but he knew he would most likely see Prince Sona again, so he could not shun him forever. His chest was so tight he felt as if it may grow too taut and snap. He could lie; after all, every ball he'd gone to

24

before was because he was obligated. His Queen had told him that his path was one of duty, and he followed it. He'd followed instructions only—business over pleasure—until that very night. Resolve had formed just enough, the urge to find someone to drag along with him peaking over his own hesitance. Lorcan was supposed to help, and yet, they were nowhere to be found. Oh, how he wished they would swoop in at that moment and save him.

But they were not there. Fen was on his own. If he lied, he was almost sure Prince Sona would be able to tell. Everyone in his life always told him he was an awful liar. He knew this about himself. He had to face the music.

"I'm… I think 'courting' is a strong word. It's more like when you go to a bar, see someone hot, and you go to get their number—whatever that's called. That's what I'm here for, but it's my first time doing it, and I just went to all the balls before because my Queen invited me." He was rushing, explaining too fast, and he wanted to hide.

Prince Sona's face stayed neutral until he finished, and then he smiled. The smile was something Fen had never seen before. He had no idea what it was, but it made him hold his breath.

The Prince spoke, his voice low, and Fen detected a note of… fear? He could not know for sure. "If that's the case, let's do this. I'm here for the first reason. I do have people I need to speak to; I'm sure you understand that, as a new vampire, I need to network a little. But, after, maybe… maybe I'll be here for the second."

Fen thought his body had turned to stone. His eyes were unable to look away from Prince Sona's, which were the warmest amber brown. He didn't know what to do or say. His face was hot, his palms were sweaty, and he didn't know how to respond anymore. He tried, and no words formed. He had to get a hold of himself, but before he could, he felt an arm wrap around his shoulders and saw a slew of bright colors out of the corner of his eye.

"Who is *this*?" Lorcan prodded, looking into Fen's face with an expression of pure amusement. "Did you get a boy's number already?"

Prince Sona regarded Lorcan with stormy eyes. For a moment, it seemed as though his annoyance returned with a vengeance, but it was quickly washed away. "Not yet, we didn't quite get that far. Who might you be?"

"Majesty Lorcan, pleasure to make your acquaintance," they said, their subtle Irish accent dripping with charm, a little

26

too thick. "I hate to do this, but my dear Prince Fen is needed elsewhere, so I'm going to have to cut this short."

Lorcan pulled at Fen, dragging him away faster than he anticipated. Shocked, Fen shook his head. "Wait! Can we just exchange numbers first? I only know his name." The next part he whispered. "You're not being a very good wing friend."

Lorcan scoffed and rolled their eyes. "Queen Eluvia asked for you, it's not my call."

Fen looked at the floor, dejected, not wanting to keep his Queen waiting, but not wanting to let this Prince go quite yet. His conflicting feelings made his stomach lurch more and more, sweaty palms worsening. What was he to do?

As he roiled in his own mind, he heard footsteps catch up and a hand grasp at his sleeve. He turned, seeing Prince Sona's face, his annoyed expression back on full display and directed at Lorcan. They returned the look, the both of them sharing a tense moment Fen felt torn between.

"It'll only take a moment."

"Sorry, he's important and needed somewhere else."

Prince Sona frowned, turning his face to Fen.

In such a quick moment that Fen could barely register, Prince Sona pulled him closer, and whispered hurriedly, "I can catch up with you later, where will you be?"

27

Flustered, but happy, Fen felt a welling of mischief bloom, a rare occurrence. It was no harm; Lorcan would just have to deal with it and whatever issues they were having on their own.

He leaned to whisper back in Prince Sona's ear to keep Lorcan from hearing and stopping him. "Here, in the castle... it's just... I live here. If I'm not in the ballroom, come to the fourth floor and look for the black door carved with bats and pomegranates. I should be there."

When Fen pulled away, Prince Sona's face was unreadable. It made Fen's heart drop, fearing he had made a mistake, but it was too late; Lorcan's patience had run out, and they dragged Fen away once again.

"Whatever you two just said to each other, it better have been worth it."

-

Fen and Lorcan made their way to Eluvia, their Queen and the owner of the castle. They both lived there, along with many of the other Royals of the house. The Queen wore a deep purple gown that showed her arms with a satin sash draped over them. It was form-fitted and had a slit down the side, revealing slim, tan legs. Her cascading black hair was slicked back and straight, not a hair out of place. Diamond earrings matched an ornate necklace and sharp diamond heels. As she inclined her head, her skin sparkled with silver glitter, just subtle enough. She looked every bit the Queen she was.

Both Royals bowed to her, a gesture only done in public with their Queen. She smiled so warmly at them that Fen felt almost all his worries and anxieties melt away, replaced by his affection for Eluvia. She gestured for him to come forward to her seat. She was perched on a gold-gilded chair, legs crossed, with a table in front of her filled with all her favorite hors d'oeuvres and wines. No one sat next to her unless she allowed it, so, as such, the table was empty of guests.

"Lorcan, you may go. Thank you for fetching Prince Fen," the Queen said, her smile still shining.

"Of course, my Queen. Please don't hesitate to let me know if you need anything else from me."

She laughed, a wonderful sound that rang like a bell. "No, my dear, enjoy yourself— it is our home after all."

Lorcan nodded, casting what looked like a concerned glance at Fen, but left before he could decipher it.

"*Mi querido*," she said softly as he sat in the seat to her right, her accent rich as caramel and just as sweet. "How does your search fare?"

Fen stared bashfully at the table, avoiding her gaze. He fidgeted with his glass, swirling around the blood inside and tapping his feet anxiously against the marble floor. "Nothing yet."

Eluvia tsked, shaking her head. "Darling, your lies are like a rainy day: easily sensed."

Fen sighed. "I just…I just started. I talked to one guy so far, so nothing much yet."

"I understand," she said. "I just worry for you. I want to ensure your happiness always, as you know. You've been talking about finding a partner. I threw this ball in hopes you would find someone that suited your tastes. I do hope tonight does not leave you wanting."

Threw the ball for him? Fen had not known that was her reasoning, and while touched by her gesture, he could not help but feel guilty.

"I think this will just take some time for me; you know how I am," Fen said, trying his best not to let his smile turn sad. "I want love, not just an arrangement."

Eluvia wrapped an arm around Fen's shoulders, pulling him closer. "I know this, my love. You take your time. I only want what you want."

"I appreciate it, I really do. Thank you."

"Are you sure you do not require my help in this matter? I know many vampires here tonight that would be suitable, to my standards at the very least, which may align with yours."

Fen knew she meant well, but she could not know what kind of person he wanted. While she was like a mother to him, she was still a true vampire, and in true vampire fashion, thought only of advantages. Her matches for him would be powerful, to be sure, but nothing more. He did not care for power; he had his fill of his own.

"No, my Queen, I promise I can manage on my own."

"Very well darling, do let me know if you need anything at all, and it will be done." She let go of Fen, allowing him to straighten up as she said, "Now, don't let me keep you any longer. Go about your night and find what you seek."

Fen flashed her as genuine a smile as he could muster, and stood to leave. He felt sick somehow, but was certain his conversation with Eluvia was not the cause. His mind kept flashing to the expression on Prince Sona's face from before, unreadable and frustrating. What had he done wrong? He thought back; no faults came to mind. Was Lorcan to blame? He did not want to begrudge his best friend, but he had a feeling there was something on their end going on, and it made him upset. He hated not knowing things and feeling like people were keeping secrets from him. Even Eluvia revealing the reason for the ball was enough to bother him. What more would he have to endure that same night?

After getting back to the main floor of the ballroom, he set his half-finished glass on a table and made his way to the exit. He dared to look around the room for Prince Sona and found him quickly. His demeanor seemed completely different than when they had spoken. With him, Prince Sona seemed expressive, perhaps even relaxed. As he watched, he saw a straight-backed man who seemed to fit just fine into the room of vampires that he felt so far away from. It pissed him off. Who was the real Prince Sona? Which was the lie? He did not want to stay any longer. Fen trod up the stairs, not bothering to look for Lorcan as he opened the door to the main hall and shut it carefully behind him. The dejected Prince would go to his room, greeted by the familiar bats and pomegranates carved into the door, and he would wait. He would get his answers.

Chapter 4

Soren

Prince Fen lives in this *castle? His Queen was* the *Queen Eluvia? What the fuck am I doing? What should I do?* Thoughts swirled in Soren's head as he did his best to act like a Royal to all the other Royals he spoke with at the ball. They were all exactly as he pictured, all sneers, passive-aggressive jabs, and lies. It reminded him why he was there in the first place. Things had gone surprisingly well. His act as "Prince Sona" worked with all the vampires, gaining him incredibly valuable information—along with some that he suspected was just gossip. His contact, whom he now had a name and face for, caused him no more trouble after the interaction with Prince Fen. When he heard Lorcan's voice, he knew immediately it was them, the Irish accent giving them away. What he didn't understand was why they were so against him speaking with Prince Fen. What were they hiding?

At that moment, Soren did not care. He was thankful for Lorcan's help with the Royals, but the longer the night went on, the more restless he became. He juggled the paths he could take with Prince Fen, a whirlwind in his mind with every breath. Soren knew he had three options. First, he could leave, never paying him a second thought and banishing The Prince's sharp and pleasing face from his mind. Second, he could attempt to ask Lorcan for more information about Prince Fen, but they still seemed touchy on the subject. Finally, the third: he could follow through, find the door Fen mentioned, and come clean. Against all his instincts, he *wanted* the third option. At the very least, he could meet with Prince Fen and convince him to join the Rogues' side, just as Lorcan had done. If Lorcan was close with him, that could help sway him even more to help—having two Royal vampires on the inside would be even better. Surely, that was why he wanted to meet with Prince Fen; no other reasons came to mind.

Lorcan spoke through the earpiece once more to Soren. Their tone, though less harsh than when Prince Fen was involved, was still not pleased. "That was the last one on my list. Unless you have any others you need to follow up with, you are free to leave."

Soren's stomach flipped. *Why?* "I have no one else. I'll make my exit."

"You'd better. Leave the earpiece inside the potted plant down the main hallway—I'll pick it up later."

"Sounds good, Lorcan."

They paused, and Soren realized it had not been the smartest move to poke at them.

"I guess since I know your name, it's fine you know mine. We're on the same side after all, even if you insisted on involving Fen."

"I did not involve him!" Soren had to stop himself from shouting as defensiveness overtook him. "He came up to me, I didn't ask him for any real information, and I thought I had been nice to him."

"I don't care. You cannot get him involved. I tried to warn you, but unfortunately for me and Fen, you're stubborn. He is…" they sighed, their voice morphing into something much more caring. "He's sensitive. He's not like the vampires here, but he's not like you either. I'll request this only one more time: leave Fen alone."

Soren considered, truly. He tried his best to understand where Lorcan was coming from. They were concerned for their friend, and didn't want him in danger. At the same time, if he was a vampire whom Queen Eluvia valued so much as to call him to her directly in the middle of the ball, he had to have one hell of a Blessing, and could surely take care of himself. He could end up being an asset to the Rogues that they sorely needed. There was that; plus, he had to admit to himself that he wanted to know more about the Prince—or, at the very least, he wanted to tell him the truth.

"He deserves to know. I lied to him, but you lied to him longer. Say the word and I'll keep your secret, but I won't keep mine from him."

There was a long pause, leaving Soren to wonder if Lorcan had disconnected and missed everything he'd said. He began walking to the exit hall, and Lorcan's voice was very soft.

"Do whatever you're going to do. I can't stop you. But just know, he is a brother to me, and if you cause him harm, I have no problem with taking revenge for his sake."

There was a static noise, and Soren figured they had taken off their earpiece. Once he shut the heavy door behind him, he did the same, wrapping the wires tightly and hiding them in his hand. He walked to the potted plant as instructed, took a look around to ensure no one saw, and deposited it.

Now, to find that door.

Chapter 5

Fen

Fen sat at his desk, oblivious to the way his legs bounced anxiously beneath him. He had tidied his room to near perfection: large velvet bed sheets pulled up, oversized pillows stacked and fluffed, and every item of decor placed meticulously, from gleaming pointed crystals on his desk to gilded black frames of art hung upon every wall. His head laid on his crossed arms, eyes shut tight and thoughts racing. What had he been thinking? The castle housed a multitude of public spaces, and yet here he was, awaiting a suitor in his own bedroom. His excuse was the ball, as the large number of vampires visiting meant even the more reclusive spaces may not have been as empty as he would've liked. He needed to speak with Prince Sona, to see him clearly, without the reverberant music and prodding eyes. And, as much as he loathed to admit, without Lorcan there to interfere.

His mind wandered to the interaction with Prince Sona from before, hoping to unravel some thread he hadn't noticed and reveal what was hidden underneath. There was a gnawing feeling within him, the idea that perhaps they somehow knew each other, and more than that, did not like one another. How could that be if what Prince Sona said was true? Lorcan rarely left the castle, the expanse of it seeming to cater to them just fine, save for the occasional excursions to clubs or shops. He did not want to believe his friend would hide their acquaintance with Sona, especially if they thought this Prince was unsuited to him —they were far too protective. Fen gritted his teeth, coming to his next theory: Prince Sona had been dishonest. He had spoken to him for mere moments, so the idea of him lying was not unreasonable.

That was why he needed to speak with him, alone. Any other reason would be unwise, he decided. He could not let the fluttering in his stomach rule him if Prince Sona came—he had to stay as composed as possible. His questions needed to be direct, if only to catch Prince Sona off guard, therefore inclining him towards honesty. *Yes, that could work*, he thought, lifting his head, eyes squinting into the light of the lamp in front of him. He blinked for a few moments, watching as a few meek raindrops pattered onto his window. Watching, eyes focused on the darkness beyond the glass, his view of the garden outside was warped by the gathering raindrops. He wondered how Prince

Sona would get home before sunrise in the rain, and worried for him.

He snapped out of it before more irrational thoughts clouded his tranquil moment. Why would it matter if Prince Sona got rained on? He would be fine, Fen was sure of it. *I could lend him an umbrella if he needed...* thought Fen as he groaned, running both hands through his hair and tugging at the ends. He watched the rain, attempting to ground himself into calmness as the rain came at a steady pace, though his heels still hit the floor again and again.

As he was just starting to lose his thoughts in the falling rain, he heard three soft raps on his door. His pulse immediately quickened and he sat up so fast his chair nearly toppled to the ground. He strode to the door, though not before glancing at himself in the full-length mirror on the wall. He was dressed the same as before, although now his hair was in a much worse state. Fumbling with nervous fingers, he smoothed where he could, but two more knocks came that made him jump, and he pulled his gaze away to focus solely on the door once again. He undid the locks, faster than he had ever done before, and twisted the handle of one of the doors downward, exceptionally quiet.

There, standing with one arm leaning against the half-closed door, was Prince Sona. He looked just as handsome as before, his face partially illuminated by the light filtering in from Fen's room, and his eyes shone like honey calcite, rich and golden. Fen could not breathe for a moment, looking up at this Prince who was smiling in a cheeky way that was on the verge of being too much for him. Prince Sona's lips parted to speak, but before he could, Fen heard footsteps from down the hall, far away, but coming closer. The last thing he wanted was for someone to see him talking with a new vampire in his private room, especially if it was Lorcan coming to check on him. He did not think Lorcan would abandon the ball so soon, but he was not in the mood to take the chance.

In one swift movement, Fen grasped the front of Prince Sona's jacket and yanked him inside, promptly shutting the door behind him. He heard Sona let out a low sound of surprise, but nothing more until the door was shut and they both regained their composure. Sona rubbed the back of his neck as he looked around, realizing that this was a bedroom and not a public meeting place. Fen felt exposed then, the reality of the situation hitting him in full force. What would Prince Sona think about him now? With horror, he registered what this situation could be taken as, and he wasn't sure how to explain to him that he wasn't interested in a one-night stand. *How else could he take it now that he's in my room? Fuck, I didn't think this through at all.*

Before Fen could hurriedly try to explain himself, Sona awkwardly put his hands in his pants pockets and shifted on his heels. "Is this... your room?"

Well, they had to start somewhere. "Yeah, I'm sorry, I could've mentioned that before but I was rushed and I thought this would be a less chaotic place to talk?" It came out like a question, though Sona did not seem phased.

"You're not wrong there," he said, his eyes looking around with purpose. "It's nice, in an incredibly vampire way."

Fen couldn't deny his love for a classical vampire aesthetic: large velvet bed, wood canopy, draping curtains, sconces disguised as candles along the dark maroon and black walls, and intricately woven rugs on the umber wooden floor. He lived in a castle, why shouldn't his room match?

"Thanks?" Fen said, his tone questioning once again.

"I did mean that as a compliment, it suits you."

A flutter surfaced, and he pushed it down as far as it could go. "You don't have to stand, feel free to sit anywhere!" Fen gestured to the plush chairs spread out across the room.

Sona's eyes fixed on twin chairs sitting in front of the fireplace on one wall of the room. He walked over without saying a word, sat in one of the plush red velvet chairs, and then patted the other, urging Fen to join him.

He obliged, trying to feel comfortable in his own room despite his racing nerves. As he sat down, his knee came dangerously close to touching Sona's. Fen became acutely aware of this, and forced his knee away to a more comfortable distance, hoping Sona would not notice.

If he did, he said nothing. Leaning back with his head resting on the chair, he turned to look at Fen. His eyes danced with the flames from the fire and Fen had to restrain himself from staring for too long. When Sona spoke, his eyebrows knitted and Fen watched as he displayed a look of... guilt?

"I have to tell you something." He paused. "Multiple things, I think."

Fen's body felt as though it was roiling in the fireplace with the logs. "I'm all ears, Prince Sona."

Shame flashed on his face. "I lied, and I wanted to say first that I am sorry about that. I wanted to meet up with you to tell you the truth."

So, Fen's suspicions were true, and Sona had lied. About what, he could not say. "Keep going, I won't know if I forgive you until I hear it all."

"That's fair. The first thing is that my name isn't Sona, I made that up. It's Soren."

Soren. Fen wished he could let it fall from his tongue to see how it felt, but he did not speak.

"I also am… not new. I've been a vampire for a while, I just haven't been to a ball before, so that could be a half-lie?"

Fen let his impulse get the better of him. "Prince… Soren," he said, holding steady eye contact with the other vampire.

He shook his head. "No, not Prince."

Fen's eyes widened, comprehension taking his air away. Soren was a Rogue? How did he get into the ball? Rogues were not allowed into Royal's homes; they were on their own, either never claimed, yearning for a place, or left alone, scorned. Which was he?

While most Royals saw Rogues as a stain upon the same ground, Fen had a spot within himself that felt empathy. He could never fully believe Queen Eluvia when she so confidently commented on the impurities of the Rogues. They were all vampires; some were just unlucky. How could they help that? Some were dangerous—he heard many accounts from members of his house regarding the Rogue group looking to take down all the Royal houses. He did not know to what end and hadn't been told when he asked, the only response being along the lines of,

43

"They're jealous. They want what we have and will kill to get it."

Fen was not afraid of Soren, though he was afraid of his answers. "So, you're a Rogue, then?"

A very small spark of relief blinked into view on Soren's face, and it tugged at Fen. "Just plain Soren is fine, we don't use titles out there."

Fen nodded. "Alright, Soren."

"I need to tell you why I was at the ball, but I need you to promise me something."

"What is it?"

"Just keep an open mind."

Fen blinked, nodding again. "Okay, I can do that."

"We talked about the two reasons vampires attend balls. I came with a goal. I don't know how much you know so I'll keep it short: Rogue vampires are going missing—enough to be very noticeable—and no one knows where they're going. I'm part of a group that's trying to find out why. We all know the Royals are the reason, we just don't have the proof yet, and I was here to get any information I could use to help."

Missing? He thinks the Royals are taking Rogue vampires off the streets? For what purpose? He couldn't wrap his mind around it fully, but did have to admit it wasn't out of the question. He knew many Royals who would kill a Rogue if they had the chance, though the Delegation had put in place long ago that the Rogues, unless posing an immediate threat, were not to be killed. There was order to things, even if it was on thin ice.

"Did you…" Fen licked his lips, gathering courage. "Did you find out anything?"

"I can't tell you."

Anger flushed Fen's cheeks, and Soren noticed.

"I'm sorry, bad way to start that sentence. I mean I can't tell you unless you agree to something, but I have to tell you something else first."

"Say it quick then because I really do not like secrets."

Soren gulped, his eyes darting away. "There is one I could tell you, but it's not exactly *mine* to tell. I want to, but I'm scared it'll cause some damage."

"I. Don't. Care." Fen replied through his teeth, patience wearing thin on Soren dancing around explanations. "Just tell me. I can handle it. We just met tonight, so you don't know me, and you don't get to decide what will or will not *damage* me."

"You're right. I would… I would like to know you, and this stuff won't help my case, I fear."

That worked on Fen, although he wasn't happy about it. Since he entered the room, Soren had this intense sincerity that

45

Fen could not ignore, making his doubts subside when he should be guarded. "Tell me. I promised I would have an open mind, so I will."

"It's about Lorcan, they're... not technically a Rogue yet, but they're on our side. They've been our inside person for a while now, and that's how I got into the ball. I didn't know it was them until they came over to us earlier, and I couldn't tell you then. Lorcan didn't want you involved in anything, so that's why they wanted to pull you away once they saw us together."

"But you still came to meet me?"

"I did."

A feeling of betrayal echoed like the sound of a bell in Fen's mind. Lorcan had kept something so big from him, never once thinking that maybe he might want to help. It felt like Lorcan didn't trust him, and that stung far worse than anything else.

"What else did they say?"

"Not a ton, but I know they didn't want you involved because of the danger. If things hadn't gone well tonight, I was supposed to get out, no matter what. Lorcan knew that, and I think they just didn't want you caught in potential crossfire. This whole thing I'm doing, that Lorcan is doing... the stakes are high, and I don't think they want you to risk yourself."

"Let me."

"Let you what?"

"Let me risk myself for fuck's sake! I am not a child, I'm a fucking vampire, same as the both of you, and I am not powerless and I am not some cowering animal in a trap. I can help!" He felt his eyes well with tears, and he blinked them back rapidly. The night was not going as he anticipated, and he hated it. He did not hate Soren for the lies. He understood why he did it, and he came clean the first chance he had. Lorcan did not. Lorcan lived in the same castle, they spent time together often and had every opportunity to say something, anything. His best friend, doing all of this, knowing vampires were going missing, knowing Fen would gladly help, and yet they had said nothing.

"I mean," Soren said, interrupting the tirade of thoughts Fen could barely contain. "I wouldn't stop you. If you really want to help, then I support that. We could use all the insiders we can."

Is that all he thought of him as? Another Royal to help along his cause? Not that he wouldn't, he just wanted to know that maybe now, for the first time, he could really and truly do something good.

Fen suddenly connected his gaze to Soren's, fiercely. He could see his amber eyes, the palest hint of a blush upon his cheeks. "I'll do it. Whatever I need to do, I will."

Soren's eyes squinted at the edges in a small smile. "I'd like that."

"Because you need all the help you can get, right?"

"That too," he shrugged.

The butterflies were back, and Fen fought them down, not wanting to ruin his confident moment. "Well, good then."

"Yeah, I'd call it good." Soren reached a hand into his jacket pocket, took out his cell phone, and held the power button until the screen lit up. "Give me your number."

Fen could not hold back the heat in his face, his voice a little too high as he said, "Oh, oh yeah! For business, I get it."

Soren handed his phone to Fen, and as he made himself a contact and entered the numbers, he was keenly aware of the other man's gaze never leaving him, his chin in his hand as he leaned on the arm of the chair. His hair came down slightly over his eyes, the red streak in it catching the firelight. It was making Fen type all the faster, trying to squirm out of Soren's unmovable look. As he handed his phone back, his fingers brushed against Soren's, and the shock nearly made him drop it. Soren caught it, shoving it back into his pocket and turning his attention back to Fen.

"It doesn't just have to be for business," he said slowly, as if to make sure Fen understood fully. "If you're okay with that."

"Yeah!" Fen replied, much too quickly. "I could text you or something, if that's what you mean."

"We could text," he said, eyes like two embers unyielding in a storm. "But I'd rather ask you out in person."

Fen's stomach could no longer hold back the flutters inside, a full hurricane sweeping him away in the giddiness of it all. Ask him out on a date? Was it too absurd? "Do you have time for that? You're like a secret Rogue spy or something, I thought you'd be too busy?"

"Even Rogue secret spies have days off," Soren said, his smile sly and far too wonderful. "So I'd like to take you out, whenever you're free."

"I... I don't have any plans tomorrow," Fen offered. "But any other day is fine too! I'm not picky!"

"Tomorrow it is." After a small pause, Soren's tone became as flirty as Fen thought it could be, and it made his head foggy. "Where would you like to go? Name a place."

Fen could return this energy, he had to, or else he would get swept up in it all and be lost. "Surprise me," he said, amazed that his voice was steady.

Soren flashed a cocky grin—one that Fen wanted to hate but couldn't; it looked too good on him. "You got it, Prince Fen."

His name sounded like black pearls dripping from Soren's voice, and the moment felt just as rare. Fen had never felt so flustered so fast by someone. It would not be his first date or potential… whatever they may become, but Soren's confidence and assertiveness were impossible to ignore. His fingertips burned, the urge to reach out so strong it was almost painful. He opted instead to let the knee he had been so carefully keeping out of reach softly brush against Soren's. It was so minor that he worried he was the only one to feel anything from it, but as they connected, Soren looked down and then back up. He had a surprised look that inspired the happiest feeling in Fen.

That momentary touch was all it took to dissuade Fen's tension, though it rose again when Soren's body started leaning. He was coming closer, and Fen did not anticipate it. He had no time to prepare, no time to gather his twittering heart and keep it steady as Soren's face came closer, his stunning features in full view. It was impulsive and fast, but he couldn't deny he wanted the closeness at that moment.

Four harsh knocks on the door rang out in their silence, the both of them startling and jumping up from their seats. Neither of them had heard anyone coming in their distracted state, and Fen began to panic. He was not ready to face anyone else, not yet. He thought about ignoring whoever it was, his finger going to his lips to shush Soren, and he nodded in agreement. They stood completely still until a voice erupted from outside the door.

"Fen, I know you're in there, you never leave your room lights on. I need to talk to you."

It was Lorcan.

Fen kept the same position, closing his eyes in a mock prayer in hopes that Lorcan would leave well enough alone.

"I will literally sit in front of your door until you open it, and I'll keep knocking until the morning comes. Let me in or I will be the most annoying person that you've ever seen."

Fen sighed, giving up. He yelled back, "Give me a second to finish changing and then I'll let you in!"

"Good, hurry it up!"

Panic reared again as Fen realized that Soren was still standing stiffly, and there was only one door. He frantically looked around, trying to come up with a hiding place for the man who was making his face burn with a permanent blush.

51

After a moment, Soren whispered, "Does the window open?"

Fen raised his eyebrows incredulously. "The *window*?"

"Yes, unless you have a secret door in here, which seems likely but you never know."

No such secret door was in his room, and he put his face in his hands. Through his fingers, he replied, "Yeah, the windows open, but it's raining and you'll get soaked!"

Fen felt hands wrap around his wrists and pull them away from his face, revealing Soren to be just inches from him, the kindest smile he had seen in many years right before his eyes. "A little water never hurt anybody."

With that and another loud knock, Fen made his way over to the windows and flung one open into the rain, watching as Soren jumped up onto the windowsill. Fen was holding it open with one hand, and Soren replaced it, grabbing Fen's hand with his free one. Fen's hand felt as though it had been struck by the lightning outside, all electricity and energy. Before he could think too much, Soren let go, and the moment passed.

"See you tomorrow." Then, he jumped out the window into the garden and into the darkness.

Chapter 6

Soren

Walking on the sidewalk under street lamps to guide his way, Soren peered at every hanging sign above his head, not wanting to miss his destination. The street was full of humans going home for the night, and some vampires just getting started with their days. Most shops were lowering blinds and turning signs, closers locking up and yawning as they went. The sun had just dipped the city into darkness when Soren left his apartment, triple-checked his phone, and then shoved his hands in his leather jacket pockets. He felt utterly ridiculous yet equally excited for his date with Fen. He could hardly believe the words himself, or his own state of mind around the other vampire. Though Fen had agreed to join the Rogue's side, he was still a Royal.

A Royal he had spent the majority of the daylight hours texting from bed, which he bristled at the realization of. Their conversation consisted of a lot of questions and answers, small talk, and trying to get to know the Prince better. His head swirled with all he had learned: his favorite color, what foods he preferred, what genre he liked to read, what activities he did in his spare time, and the fact that he liked silver over gold. All of it felt so mundane, so simple in the grand scheme of things. Here he was, his main hobby trying to take down the Royals and get to the bottom of Rogue disappearances, and he was now eagerly awaiting getting a coffee with Prince Fen.

Prince Fen was everything Soren knew the Royals were not. He admitted he cried at sad movies, hated the idea of miscommunications in romances, and was painfully sincere in everything he did. Somehow, in the turning of him becoming a vampire and the years that followed, he had stayed so… human. He'd said coming to terms with drinking blood was (or had been) difficult for him, being a vegetarian in his past life now needing blood to survive. Though he said he had made peace with it, so long as the blood was provided without him harvesting it himself. He'd explained that he could not bear to put another living thing in pain just for his pleasure, and in a moment of shock, Soren wondered in that moment, *what if it was my blood in offering?*

Soren blushed at the thought. Drinking another vampire's blood was an intimate act, one meant to be between lovers. At the very least, consent to feed must be given, and here he was, thinking of how Fen would react if he offered his blood to the Prince.

Shaking his head to clear his thoughts, Soren stopped suddenly as he saw the sign for the coffee shop above his head. He turned, peering into the windows of the warmly lit space, all comfortable cushions upon wooden chairs and plants hanging from every corner. String lights spanned the ceiling, and art in antique frames crowded the walls. He saw the large menu, handwritten in chalk, partly obscured by the few nightly baristas bustling about. His eyes scanned all the tables, seeing that the place was fairly populated, though thankfully not too much. As he pushed the glass door open and the bell chimed upon his entering, he spied Fen in a corner booth.

Fen's hair was different from when he attended the ball. Instead of being down and more styled, his hair was now half-up, half-down with a small ponytail and pieces of side bangs by his ears. His outfit was much less stereotypically vampiric as he sported black ripped jeans, ankle boots, and a thick forest green sweater that was a size too big for him, showing a good deal of his neckline. He looked like the exact kind of person who would ask for a cafe date, and Soren smiled at the thought, crossing the room to take a seat in front of Fen.

When he sat, he saw Fen gripping a clear plastic cup with both his hands, the iced coffee resting on the table. In front of his drink was another plastic cup, this one filled with green liquid that made Soren's chest tighten. *Matcha, he ordered my drink for me*, he thought fondly, *he remembered*. His hand drifted to the cup and he took a sip, watching as Fen's face turned up from his intense stare at his own drink, his eyes widening.

"Soren!" he said, smiling such a bright smile that his small fangs poked out from beneath his top lip and his eyes squinted. He looked perfect. His green eyes bore into him all the more, black eyeliner smokey along his lids.

"That's me," he replied, being as casual as he could manage.

Fen giggled softly, lifting his cup so the straw rested on his bottom lip. "I'm glad. That you agreed to meet here, I mean." He took a sip of his coffee and Soren could not look away. "It's my favorite spot, especially because they cater to vampire hours."

"It's nice, very cozy. Thank you for getting my drink, by the way."

"I hope you like it. I got the vanilla bean flavor in it too. I remember you saying that was something you liked?"

Right again. "Yeah, it's good, I'll have to come here more I think."

They both sat in silence for a moment, Fen clearly becoming self-conscious as his smile faded and eyes broke contact. He bit his lip slightly before looking back to Soren, though his eyes were trained on his drink rather than his face. "Can I ask you something?"

Soren, vaguely confused, responded, "Um, yeah, what is it?"

Fen's mossy eyes flitted up, a spark of courage showing. "I get wanting to find out what's going on with the Rogues," he started, voice hushed. "But why do you hate the Royals so much? And if you do... why do you seem so... okay with *me*?"

Soren stiffened. He had not thought Fen would ask anything like that; he thought he could get away with a night of not thinking about the Royals and all his distaste for them. He wanted to forget Fen was one, and he had until now. Wishful thinking, he supposed.

"I talked to Lorcan," he admitted, looking down at the table. "After the ball, I mean. They asked about the mission, and about you."

"What did you say? What did they say?" Fen pressed.

Soren considered how to answer that, thinking back to his texts with Lorcan the day before.

Lorcan had followed up, asking him if he reported everything to the other Rogues or if they should write the report. Writing grating intel was not his favorite activity, so Soren had told them to do it instead. During that time, his doubts began to form into an ugly thing. His whirl of emotions for Fen when they met had fled and been replaced with the paranoia of having made a terrible mistake. Around Fen, his guard had all but dropped, that charming face of his making him forget who he was, and making him think of all he did not know. They had only spoken briefly, his instincts in Fen's room almost overtaking him when they were in front of the fireplace, and he hadn't thought about who Fen was to Queen Eluvia. He had agreed to a date with a Prince; a Prince who decided to join the Rogues seemingly on a whim, a vampire that the most formidable Queen he knew kept close. There was more to Fen, and before meeting with him, he had to find out.

> **Soren:** *I need to ask you something.*
> **Royal Contact (Lorcan):** *What?*
> **Soren:** *I know you have a sore spot about Fen, but I need more information on him.*

Royal Contact (Lorcan): *No, I don't think you do. I told you to leave him out of all this.*

Soren: *Just because he's your friend? Isn't he Blessed? Can't he take care of himself?*

That had been the right set of questions. It was enough to poke at Lorcan and make them more impulsive and defensive, their temper getting ahead of them.

Royal Contact (Lorcan): *You don't know him like I do, you don't know what he's been through and what still haunts him. His Blessing is not something he wants to use, ever, so drop that. Besides, he's Queen Eluvia's favorite, she keeps him in that castle to make sure he's around if she needs him. If you take him away from her, I can't say anything good will happen to you.*

Soren: *He can leave on his own, it's not like I'd force him.*

Royal Contact (Lorcan): *He's too caring about everything and everyone. If you told him you needed him to join the*

Rogues to keep you from getting a damn cold, he'd do it.

Soren: *It's too late anyway.*

The next text came in with all the malice Soren knew was behind the screen.

Royal Contact (Lorcan): *What the FUCK do you mean?*

Soren: *I talked to him, told him everything. He said he would help. I just wanted to make sure we could trust him fully. He is a Royal, and you're the only other one I know on our side. I gave him the benefit of the doubt since he's your friend, but I need you to tell me if he can actually help, or if he'll just fuck us over like Royals love to do.*

Royal Contact (Lorcan): *Soren, Fen is too good for you. He's too good for anyone in this godforsaken place. He would probably be the most valuable tool for the Rogues they could ever get, and he's easy to convince. But I will beg you if I have to, don't make him a plaything for the*

Rogues. If he already agreed to help, then his mind is set, but you will keep him safe if I can't. Help him on missions, let him think he's being useful, but do not make him use his Blessing. Do not do that to him if you have any kind of conscience.

His Blessing? Curiosity clawed at Soren's mind. If Lorcan was right about Queen Eluvia valuing Fen so much, his Blessing had to be something truly incredible. He wanted to know, but he knew better than to ask. Lorcan already told him all he needed to know, for now. Enough to convince him that maybe he could go on the date, and not feel too conflicted over Fen being a Royal. If Lorcan could help, Fen could as well.

As Soren blinked back into the present moment, he looked back at Fen, sitting in front of him in all his anxious beauty. His leg was bouncing under the table, and his eyebrows were drawn down in waiting. Being in front of this man was like being stripped down to his bare emotions, his long grudge and seeded hatred all but gone looking into Fen's eyes. It was perplexing, and it was freeing.

"To sum it up, I asked Lorcan if I could trust you. I trust them, but they're the only Royal I even half-trust since they came to the Rogues themselves. They're your best friend, so I knew they'd tell me if you *could* help, and if you'd be honest."

"Okay," Fen breathed in relief, shoulders becoming a bit less tense. "That makes sense, but why do you hate the Royals so much? Were you ever in a house?"

Soren became still, channeling all his composure into keeping his memories in the back of his mind. "No, I wasn't in a house. That's all I want to say about it though, maybe... maybe some other time."

Fen's look softened. His free hand twitched, and it moved an inch towards Soren, but he quickly pulled it back. "That's okay, thank you for telling me, we don't have to talk about this stuff anymore if you don't want to. It's your day off after all!"

And just like that, Fen shifted the energy back into what it had been at the start, coffee talk and shy glances. Maybe that was his Blessing, being able to ease Soren's nerves almost like taming a coiled snake.

"I do have another question though," Fen said, a familiar blush tinting his cheeks.

Soren rolled his eyes, taking a few sips of his drink. "Go on."

"Please tell me if I imagined it and don't be afraid of embarrassing me because I already am for asking about this, and if you also don't want to talk about this that's fine it's just been on my mind and I hate not knowing so..."

He was rambling. It was cute.

"So I've just been thinking about when we were in front of the fireplace in my room and it kind of felt like you leaned forward and you were gonna..." Fen trailed off again, the red in his face blooming while he spoke until it was like a rose on full display.

Soren's face wasn't much better. When they were in Fen's room, all he had seen were Fen's mesmerizing forest eyes, pretty face lit by the fire, dressed in his romantically vampiric ball attire, all while he had seemed so timid and gentle. His own blush bloomed, his usually confident persona cracking. He had no idea what to say; he wished he could take back leaning towards Fen in a moment of weakness, drawn in by his hypnotizing aura that even now had him wanting more. Should he come up with an excuse? Laugh it off somehow? He could not tell the truth, that much was certain, it would be too damning to let Fen know he had caught him.

As he was juggling a million options to cover himself, Fen spoke again.

"Actually, I'm sorry, forget it! I've already grilled you tonight, I should've given you more of a break, you don't have to say anything!"

Soren let out the breath he had been holding. He was saved, he could let it go and keep his dignity intact for now, all from the mercy of the man in front of him, gulping down a latte and not realizing how beautiful he was.

Both of their drinks were starting to run out, straws gathering what little liquid was left at the bottom of the cups. They kept talking, words flowing easily like satin through fingers, Soren in those moments worrying about nothing but the next words Fen would say to him, and whether or not he could tell how Soren was hanging on every word. Even at the lulls in their conversation, it felt comfortable.

In one of those quiet moments, Soren had glanced around the room, spying a shelf lined with board games and decks of cards, other cafe patrons using the ones that were missing, and he had an idea.

"Give me a second," Soren said, and Fen's head tilted.

Soren strode over to the shelf, finding a ceramic bowl full of dice of all different colors and sizes. Rifling through them, his eyes finally rested on a deep red one for Fen, and a dark

64

green one for himself. He would not mention his color choice being related to Fen's eyes.

Sitting back down at the table, he handed the red die over to Fen, his black painted nails unfurling to open his palm to receive it. "What's this for?"

"We're playing a game," Soren said simply, pulling out his phone to open a notepad on the screen.

Fen's eyes lit up, eagerness oozing from him that was impossible not to feel as well. "I love that idea! What game?"

"Just a simple one, I don't feel like thinking too hard tonight."

Fen laughed, and Soren smiled.

"I like that idea too. Explain it to me?"

"We each have a die, and you can either write on paper or in your phone numbers one through six. Each number will be a question, or a dare for the other person. Whatever you roll coincides with what the other person wrote for you."

"So like truth or dare with dice?"

"Exactly, you already have the hang of it."

Fen began furiously typing on his phone, writing and erasing at equal paces, and Soren wondered already what Fen would have in store for him. He wrote his own, keeping them simple and sweet, enough to keep him from losing any more control than he had already relinquished to Fen that night. Once they were done, they both placed their phones face down on the table to keep the other from seeing.

"Who goes first?" asked Fen.

"The rule is the prettiest person goes first, so roll."

Fen's face flushed and he cleared his throat. "Okay, if you wanted me to go first you could've just asked."

"I'm just sticking to the rules."

Fen shook his head slightly, picking up his die and tossing it onto the table. Their game was now under way.

Chapter 7

Fen

The moon shone blearily through the foggy sky, street lamps gathering moths in droves, wings silently keeping them in the light's gaze. Metal benches sat facing the thin river to Fen and Soren's side, the bank blocked by a fence all down its border. The sidewalk was underfoot, and the subject of Fen's attention at the moment, as he found it impossible to look Soren in the face for too long. The butterflies in his stomach would not cease no matter his actions to subdue them, the presence of the other man next to him like a tidal wave pressed against glass, barely holding back from breaking. Their conversation flowed with ease, the night air warm around them, Soren's hands in his pockets and his pace steady, keeping time with Fen. That was all the better, as the urge to grab his hand, while logically sound, would only further Fen's nervousness. Taking a walk together after being at a cafe felt so utterly *normal*. It had been well over twenty years since he had done anything similar—not since he was a human—and it infected his mind with the thought of it all being too good to be true. He silently thanked Soren that the only dare he had written for him in their dice game was to take a walk together. If only that moment—the two walking side by side—silly comments and little questions, would last for another twenty years.

Fen dared to peek up at Soren's face, and to his surprise, their eyes met, Soren gazing at him with such fondness it was blinding. They both tore their eyes away at once, looking in the opposite direction. Their voices went shaky before Soren quickly recovered, Fen staying silent for fear of exposing his rapidly beating heart if he spoke. Soren had been looking at him with an expression Fen could scarcely believe was for him. He wished the moment would last as long as memory could hold.

"How far is your castle from here?" Soren asked, changing the subject of whatever they had been talking about, which Fen had forgotten after their exchanged looks.

"We've been walking towards it this whole time, we're maybe halfway there?"

"Am I allowed to walk you home, or is the Prince keeping me a secret from the Queen?" Soren teased.

Fen smiled. "I probably should go back on my own, but we can keep walking for a while longer if you want?"

"I wouldn't hate that," Soren said. "As long as you'll have me."

How Fen wished he could. Before letting that thought spread, Fen nodded, trying to clear his head. "Yeah, I'm okay with that."

They kept at their leisurely pace, the castle's spires looming in the distance and growing ever closer. Fen did not want to keep Soren a secret from Eluvia, in fact, it was rather difficult not to knock on her door and gush that he had finally found a suitor. He knew she would be happy for him, if only Soren were a Prince. He didn't think Queen Eluvia hated Rogues; if anything, she seemed neutral, but the Delegation had rules that even she had to follow if she wanted to stay in their good graces. Rogues must be avoided, unless they were accepted into a house. Some Royals hated them, but did they hate them enough to kidnap them? Fen knew it was possible. Eluvia was a vampire Queen, powerful and intimidating to anyone she met, but she was also the closest thing Fen had to a mother in many years. It hurt to keep his life so private from her now, when before he was nothing but open. He hated secrets, and yet here he was with some of his own.

He could tell Lorcan, but he had the suspicion that they would like it even less. Fen felt overwhelming dejection all at once, realizing he had no one to speak to regarding his feelings, or about Soren. He gained support after becoming a vampire when he had lost it all before, and it had been wonderful. Now, he felt isolated, his thoughts trapped with no one to let them out. Fen clenched his hands, nails biting into his palms, and the pain grounded him. Lorcan would warm up eventually, he was sure, and then he could discuss with them all he wanted. He just had to wait.

"Fen?" Soren spoke, his fingers resting on Fen's shoulder, yanking him from his thoughts.

He hadn't realized he was silent, Soren speaking into the air with no response. "Sorry," said Fen, his fingers unfurling. "I think I just was in my own head for a second there, what were you saying?"

"We're getting closer to the castle, I just wanted to make sure I left before anyone saw."

The words stung, though he knew Soren did not mean them to. He did not want to hide, but he knew he had to if he wanted this happiness to last longer than two nights. And he did, so very badly.

"You're right, you should probably head back now," Fen replied, doing his best to give Soren a comforting smile.

Soren's brows furrowed in concern, his hand still lingering on his shoulder. "Are you okay?"

Fen wasn't, but the hand resting on him was enough to tide him over, at least for now. He figured his moment of bravery could last a bit longer. He reached his own hand up, resting it on Soren's and squeezing his fingers. The heat of their hands together was the only thing Fen wanted to feel, and he let himself, looking up at Soren's beautiful amber eyes. He gazed for a long moment that felt frozen, and he wanted it to be burned into his memory, overwriting his negativity from before. It was working, and although the feelings still itched at the back of his mind, he let this be at the forefront.

"I am, don't worry about it. Thanks for going out with me, I had a really, really good time."

Soren squeezed Fen's hand back, shooting electricity all down Fen's arm. "I'll believe you, for now at least."

They both retracted their hands, and Fen felt the cold they left in their wake, already missing the warmth. He took a step back, trying to distance his body before he could do anything more, anything at all to feel that heat again. "Well, I guess I'll see you later?" He paused, then amended, "Only if you want to, that is."

Soren chuckled, and the sound was like the sweetest of honey that Fen wanted to taste over and over. "I'd like to. Text me anytime, and I'll let you know when I'm free. After all, you're the damsel in his tower with nothing else to do, right?"

Fen blushed, hating that he was technically right. He spent his days mostly on hobbies, talking to Lorcan, maybe helping Queen Eluvia with documents from time to time. He liked his simple, quiet life, and here was Soren, disrupting it all. His life was becoming a tempest, one he would gladly be swept away by, so long as Soren was the one causing the storm.

"And what if I am busy, huh?"

"Then I'll sneak in. Just keep the window open." Soren winked, and it sent a fierce blush that Fen could feel spread to his ears. Fen needed to get his revenge somehow; he couldn't be the only one flustered and losing his cool.

Fen, looking only at Soren's left hand at his side, reached out as quickly as only a vampire could, and brought the hand up to his face. He pressed his lips against Soren's hand, and just as quickly released it, looking up at his face in triumph. It had worked, as the hand he had kissed was hanging in the air, Soren's eyes wide, lips parted in shock and cheeks flushed. Before Soren could do anything, Fen turned on his heel and began walking—practically marching—away, only looking back to address the Rogue.

"I'll text you when I'm home, try not to think about me too much!"

Fen walked as fast as he could without running back to the castle, his heart beating so hard and fast, and it was lovely.

Chapter 8

Soren

Soren's hand felt like it was inlaid with fireworks the rest of the night, his eyes half shut as he lay on his stomach in bed. He had only taken his shoes off before falling onto his bed, thoughts racing and hand aching. He had to change and get ready to sleep for the day, but his mind wouldn't stop replaying the night, especially the ending. He tore his eyes away, though begrudgingly, to pull his phone out of his pocket. No text yet. He would wait as long as it took; that's what a good date would do. It was his duty. He would not sleep until he heard that Fen returned safely home, and not just because his heart yearned to see him again as soon as possible.

He sighed, laying his phone with the screen up on his bed. The least he could do while waiting was change. While tearing himself off the sheets, he stood and took off his jacket, followed by the rest of his clothes until he wore only long pajama pants, and walked back over to the bed. Still no text. What was he doing, waiting with bated breath for a text he did not know would be coming anytime soon, or at all? What if Fen decided dating a Rogue was too much trouble? Lorcan could have convinced him that Soren was bad news... What then? He flopped down onto his pillows, staring at the ceiling fan spinning above him lazily. He was being paranoid, and it made him self-conscious. No one else made his mind race with possibilities; Fen was at the center of it all. Here he was, alone in his studio apartment, just some vampire off the streets pining for a powerful Prince up in a castle ruled by the most respected vampire Queen.

What was happening to him?

As his thoughts only swirled faster, the vibration of his phone lit up the room much brighter than his small bedside lamp, and his chest seized. Soren grabbed the phone in a rush, opening the text message Fen had just sent. The words set his mind at ease, the storm in his mind settling, and he focused just on those words.

Fen: *Home now! :)*

Soren pondered for a moment, wondering how far he should push the moment, how far he should let his emotions get the better of him. It was clear to him that Fen at least felt something for him, but during the date, there was a moment of worry, and all Soren wanted was to make it better. Seeing Fen's face deep in thoughts unknown to Soren made him feel something he could not place. He wanted to know, but didn't want to ruin what they had going on. He could settle for other means of pushing Fen.

Soren: *How do I know for sure?*

A moment later, another message popped up, though this one was a picture. There was Fen, smiling into the camera in a large sleep shirt that hung a bit off one shoulder, showing his bare skin, large velvety pillows in the background that were clearly from his bed. His smile was so wide, his fangs just visible and his eyes completely closed. He was the most gorgeous thing Soren could ever remember seeing.

Fen: *Here's proof! :P*

Another text popped up before Soren could respond.

Fen: *Where's the proof that you got home safe and sound? ;)*

His heart skipped. Fen was far more bold over text than in person, without his constant blushing to give him away.

Soren opened the camera function on his phone, remembered he was shirtless, and promptly took a picture of himself, making sure his lack of a shirt was obvious, and sent it. Lying on his side, phone resting on the pillow just inches from his face, he stared at the picture Fen had sent and wondered if he was allowed to save it. Should he ask? He decided not to, at least for now.

A response popped up, and it made Soren laugh.

Fen: *Okay wow, I don't think I know if I have a response for that. I should've thought before I asked, was that weird? That's a really good picture of you though, I can see your tattoos really well! Sorry, that might be weird to say too. Stop me anytime! Please!*

So he rambles in text too when he's flustered, good to know, Soren thought. He wanted to push his luck. He wanted to forget about his missions, the Royals, and Fen being a Prince, and just for the rest of the night, he wanted to text the boy he liked.

Soren: *I won't stop you. In fact, save the picture if you like it so much, I don't mind.*

Fen: *Ditto. I mean, to the picture I sent you! Lol!*

Soren's smile began to make his cheeks ache. He scrolled back up to Fen's picture, saved it to his phone, and sat there for a moment, just looking at that beautiful, smiling face, before going back to text Fen for as long as they could both stay awake.

He sighed.

He was so fucked.

Chapter 9

Fen

With nothing but the sound of echoes in the corridor, Fen fidgeted with the ends of his sleeves and thought only of worst-case scenarios. He had spoken to Eluvia in passing since the ball, joining her for rushed meals before she had to leave and do whatever her duties entailed, but now she was formally summoning him. To what end, he did not know, and his paranoid thoughts only grew with each step closer to her study. Never had he been so anxious to see her; it was usually all warmth and comfort, but now for the first time, he had something to hide. Now he had Soren. Soren the Rogue vampire, all deep brown hair and tattooed arms and the smell of cedar. Fen thought of all the things Eluvia could say. Would she tell him not to see Soren anymore? He could not stomach the thought.

What was more, as his jaw was hard set and starting to ache, he heard rapid footsteps behind him. He turned his head, spying Lorcan rushing after him, their freckled face scrunched in caution. Ever since Fen had started seeing Soren more and more, Fen had kept his thoughts to himself more often than not. They still spoke and spent plenty of time together, but he felt it better not to disturb the peace they had with any talk of Soren and his honeyed eyes and frequently changing streak of hair that had been red, but last Fen saw it had been green instead. He wanted so badly for his friend to be just that: a friend, someone to confide in and speak to about anything on his mind, especially the biggest thing clouding his thoughts. Lorcan had a sour look on their face anytime Soren was even alluded to, and the longer it went on, the more it hurt.

His face must have shown his anxiety clear as day, as when Lorcan neared, their expression turned to soft concern. "Hey," they said, putting their hands in the pockets of their jeans, blue eyes staring directly into Fen's face. "What's got you all nervous?"

His fingers toyed with the sleeves of his thick sweater, the fabric feeling suffocating all of a sudden. "Eluvia asked me to come see her."

"That's not usually something you don't like," Lorcan replied, eyebrows knitting together in confusion. "Do you think she's upset at you or something?"

Fen shrugged, trying to act nonchalant. "She could be."

Lorcan scoffed. "She could never be mad at her golden boy, it's something else, isn't it? Spill!"

His temper was rising and he hated it. He didn't want to snap at Lorcan, but his emotions were high and his patience was running thin. Fen either had to leave, or let his words out however they were meant to. "Lorcan, I honestly don't think you *want* to know." His tone was harsh, despite his attempt at holding it back. *Shit.*

Their face faltered a moment, and Fen could see it, and it stung. "I do, I wouldn't have asked otherwise. You've never had issues being honest before, what's the problem?"

It was coming. The words he so desperately wanted to keep on his tongue, better bottled within himself than flung at his friend. They were his true feelings, and he didn't want them to hurt Lorcan, but keeping it all inside was something he never wanted to do, not with them. It was his last chance to use an excuse to get out, to put this off for as long as he could just like he had been doing all this time. Weeks had gone by since meeting Soren, blissful, wonderful weeks he couldn't share with anyone else. He hadn't told Lorcan about their first date at the cafe, about the dice game, the walk together, the many nights of Soren sneaking in the window so they could talk all night, of the countless texts and inside jokes they shared, and he couldn't show the beautiful pictures of the beautiful boy he was getting to know better and better with each passing day. The wave of it all

81

hit him, and he felt his eyes turn damp as he could not force them to meet Lorcan's.

"You want me to be honest?" Fen asked through gritted teeth, voice just beginning to shake.

Lorcan did not respond for a moment, the silence allowing Fen to feel just how heavy his chest felt, until they broke it. "Is it about Soren?"

Uttering his name had spilled the last amount of control Fen had on the ground, for Lorcan's voice had said his name with a bitterness Fen could not allow, not from his friend. As he began speaking, he focused on keeping his voice steady and low enough not to echo his feelings down all the hallways of the castle.

"No, Lorcan, it's about you. All that time you worked with the Rogues, and you never told me. I can help, and Soren saw that right away without barely even knowing me, but my friend of what, twenty years didn't even think to ask? I could've let that go, I could've gotten over that so quickly it wouldn't have mattered, but then the way you make me feel when I talk about Soren makes me so, so sad, Lorcan. That's what I feel is *sad*. You are my best friend, one of the few vampires I have ever met who makes me feel okay, and I... I find someone, after all this time, and you treat even the thought of him like some disgusting thing you need to turn away from. And I just can't understand *why*, why you wouldn't be happy for me, let me tell you all about him, let me share that part of my life with you because I care about you. I've spent twenty-five years as a vampire, and you've known me for almost all of them. And now, for the first time, it feels like you think of me completely different than how I thought you did, when my feelings towards you never changed. Why?"

Fen could feel a few small tears run down his cheeks, and he wiped them away as quickly as they came. His words could not be taken back, and he feared what their consequences might be. He could lose his best friend. He never wanted to lose anyone again and here he was, causing his own pain. Fen blinked away his tears, looking at Lorcan's face for the first time since his outburst. He could not have braced himself for the heartbroken look on their face. It was equal parts guilt and concern, their fists clenched at their sides, and they took a deep breath. Fen almost flinched when they started to reply, anticipating the worst.

"I'm… I'm sorry."

What?

"You're just so… sensitive, Fen. I thought you'd grow out of that after joining a Royal house, that you'd fit in a little more after everything that happened. But you've stayed the exact same. Vampires get diluted over time into nothing, the human parts of them gone. You're always emotional and honest and I want more than anything to keep you that way. You're my best friend too, and who you are is so special. That's why I couldn't bring myself to ask you for your help with the Rogues, or why I never thought Soren could be good for you. Your Blessing is nothing like what anyone else has, and there is always that chance someone will exploit you for it. I want you to help the Rogues, but I want you to be safe. I knew right away Soren would ask you to help, and that I couldn't stop him, but I wasn't going to be happy about it. So, I'm sorry. I didn't know you felt all that, and I'm sorry you kept everything to yourself all this time. I can't say you seeing Soren makes me overjoyed, but as long as he keeps you safe, I can at least sleep a little easier."

Fen had listened intently to Lorcan, their smooth and steady voice grounding him. He understood, in an objective way. He didn't want the Rogues to take advantage of him either, but he wasn't weak; he was still a vampire and he wanted to help. He would help. And Soren… Soren wouldn't do anything like that. If keeping him safe was what had to be done to get Lorcan to be more comfortable with the idea, so be it. It was a step in the right direction, and it made Fen hopeful that things could be exactly how he wanted them to be. He could have Lorcan as his best friend, and Soren as his… as his.

Fen gave Lorcan a very small smile, his emotions still shaky but solid enough. "I accept your apology."

His friend returned the smile, then ran a hand through their hair, trying to dispel the tense atmosphere. "So, I guess if you need someone to be all mushy to, my door is open."

"I might take you up on that," Fen said. "If Eluvia doesn't ban me from seeing him or something."

"You think that's what she asked you to her study for?" Lorcan asked, incredulous. "She's not going to stomp on your happiness, I know that for a fact."

Fen sighed, relaxing his hands and turning his head to glance towards Eluvia's door. "Guess I'll find out."

-

"Come in," Queen Eluvia called, her melodic voice lessening Fen's anxiety, if only slightly. She sounded as laid back as ever, which was a good sign.

He opened the door, spotting her sitting in a high-backed chair at an ornate wooden desk, intricately carved with various leaves and blooms. Two crystalline table lamps illuminated the space in front of her, a sleek laptop just being closed as he shut the door behind him. She looked as beautiful as she always did, which Fen always wondered how she could manage. Her long hair was pulled up tightly in a ponytail that hung down her back, and a satin button-up blouse the color of an eggplant matched a sparkling eyeshadow that popped amidst the rest of her dark eye makeup. Her brown skin was dewy and perfect, the shine of it catching the light as she sat back in her seat, a gentle smile on her lips.

"My dear," she gestured to the chair ahead of him that faced her. "Sit. Do you need anything? A drink?"

Fen took his place, most of his nerves calmed, though a prickle still dwelled on the back of his neck. "No, thank you though!" He had been too cheery, she would notice.

Eluvia chuckled softly, shaking her head. "My darling boy, I did not mean to cause unease by calling you here, though I suppose being in my study, it does feel a bit formal."

Fen nodded, and swallowed.

"I will be quick, then you can get back to smiling at your phone if that is what you desire."

Fen's face snapped up, his cheeks growing hot as he looked at Eluvia, a teasing smile on her lips. She knew he was at least talking to someone, did she know who? He had as much freedom as he wanted, but he still hadn't gone to Soren's home yet, just in case someone saw him there and spoke to her. He had to be the one to tell her, if he ever did. He wanted to, he knew she would be happy for him, but Soren being a Rogue was not a part of her plan for him, and he feared disappointing her. She wanted him with another Royal, a powerful one who would join their house and strengthen it. Fen had never given it much thought, not until now. How would she react? He wasn't prepared to find out, not after the emotional toll speaking with Lorcan had been.

He decided to be playful about it, but still vague. "You noticed?" He asked sheepishly.

"Of course, I always notice how you are feeling. As long as they are making you happy, I see no problem."

Relief washed over him.

"Although, you will need to introduce me at some point."

The nerves were back.

"Take your time, my love, I am willing to wait for you to determine when the time is right."

Fen felt like his emotions were on a horrid carriage ride, being thrown about in every direction. He would at least breathe a bit easier for the time being, but the inevitable still nagged at his mind. "Of course, I just need more time."

Eluvia nodded and rested her chin on her hands as she propped her elbows on the table. "That is not why I asked you here, if you'll forgive my changing the subject. I merely wanted to let you know I will be away for several days. I tell you this so you do not wonder where I am."

She was leaving? To where? When? Fen had many questions, as she only left the castle very rarely, especially for days at a time. He wanted to ask every question, but did not want to seem like a desperate child clinging to his mother. He felt a pang of loneliness at that thought.

"Dear Fen, I can see your thoughts like a pond of ravenous fish, so eager for more." She laughed. "Do not fret. I am visiting another Royal house on business assigned by the Delegation, nothing more. It is sure to be dull, and I should not be away for more than one week's time."

That all made sense; she was one of the more prestigious vampires and the Delegation always had something for her to do. He understood, and told Eluvia as such before she dismissed him, stating she had more work to be done in preparation for her leave. Fen loved her like a mother, and would miss her while she was away. That was fact, and yet another fact remained just as true. While he would miss her, that meant, if he could work up the courage, a visit to Soren's home would be possible. It made his heart flutter as his hand reached into his pocket to retrieve his phone. It had been off, as he'd wanted nothing to interrupt his time with Eluvia, so he waited impatiently while it powered on.

The screen flashed on, and a text notification popped up on the screen.

Soren: *How'd the meeting go, handsome?*

Fen could not hide the large smile spreading on his face, any and all nerves pushed away by one simple text. As he typed back, he rushed back to his room, wanting the comfort of Soren's voice as soon as possible.

Fen: *Can you call in a second? I'm almost back to my room.*

Soren: *Just say when.*

Fen walked as fast as his legs could carry him without breaking into a run, excitement coursing through his veins as his hand pushed open the carved wooden door to his room, shutting and locking it behind him. He checked his reflection in the mirror, making sure he was presentable enough for Soren, though it was hard to ever think he looked quite good enough for someone like him. His large red and black striped sweater would have to be enough, though he did massage down some stray hairs here and there.

Fen: *Okay, ready! :)*

The phone rang, and Fen accepted the call so fast he barely managed to lie down, arm outstretched in front of him as he lay on his stomach, shoving a pillow beneath his chin. The camera came on, and showed Soren in all his beauty on the screen. His hair was the same as always, middle-parted and messy in a good way, the new green streak vibrant, his sharp face softened in a fond expression that made Fen's chest squeeze. He smiled back.

"So," Soren began. "Tell me all about it, I thought maybe you wouldn't make it there alive with how nervous you were, I wouldn't put it past you to keel over from anxiety."

Fen rolled his eyes. "Shut up, I have a lot to say and you'll have to let me yap for a while."

"I'll gladly listen to your voice."

He felt a shiver run down his spine. Soren's flirts never failed and it annoyed him; it was maddening to have someone make his mind and body feel things he hadn't in a very long time, and he didn't know what to do.

"I have a question first, though," said Fen, attempting to build suspense.

"Oh? What is it?"

Fen bit his lip, hoping it didn't feel too awkward in the moment, but he was too late to stop. "I was just wondering, totally fine if not, I don't want you to feel pressured or anything, please be honest if it's no, I won't be hurt or anything–"

"Fen! You're starting to make *me* nervous, just ask."

He was rambling; he had to quit that habit, but Soren brought it out of him. He took a moment to breathe, bracing himself. "Do you think sometime this week I could maybe come over? To your place?"

Fen could barely bring himself to look at Soren's face through the screen, awaiting his answer that he dreaded might be no.

"Yeah," Soren said, his shell of confidence just so slightly chipped, the missing piece replaced by what sounded like hope. "You can come over whenever you want, I'd... Yeah, I'd like that."

Fen feared his smile would break from his cheeks, and as his joy refused to fade, he told Soren about his day, including the conversation with Lorcan. He thought in those moments that perhaps that was what true contentment felt like.

Chapter 10

Soren

The cold air of the open refrigerator prickled on Soren's skin as he grabbed a blood box, popped open the spout, and began chugging it. The liquid was thick and frigid going down his throat, and he drank it all as fast as his body would allow. Having little time to prepare for his date reminded him he hadn't satisfied his thirst for days, and he knew he needed to satiate himself before Fen arrived. The last thing he wanted was to feel sluggish for the first night Fen came to him, and he could not risk his craving morphing into something more… private. They hadn't seen each other in person for a while, mostly texts and calls, as Soren was busy discussing his next outing on behalf of the other Rogues. For the first time since joining the group, he felt nervous. He wanted so badly to ask Fen to come with, to help him see possibly the most important piece of the puzzle, and to do it together. Against his own urges, he could not help but think of Lorcan's words from before. Fen could take care of himself, but was it right for Soren to put him in a position where he needed to?

Downing the last of the blood in the paper carton, Soren tossed it into the trash can. The timing of the mission could not have been worse. Queen Eluvia was gone on some Royal business trip, leaving Fen's schedule wide open to do anything he desired, and he had hoped to be a part of those plans. The mission was of dire importance, a team of at least five other vampires agreeing to it, and he had made up his mind to ask Fen along. He could protect himself, and in the event he couldn't, at least Soren would be there. Over time, he had shared as many details as he could with Fen, but even Soren had not been privy to the details of this mission. They wanted to keep it all quiet until day-of, and he just hoped it was worth it. It had to be.

As Soren made his way to his bed to lie down and overthink some more, he heard the softest of knocks echo from his apartment door and a text notification buzz from his phone.

Fen: *I'm here :)*

Panicked, he spun on his heel, looking around frantically to make sure everything was in order. He had cleaned and made his modern studio look as nice as he could manage, and he just hoped Fen would like it, though it was much more of this century than his usual tastes. He held up his phone and gazed into the camera, checking his hair and face as he walked to the door. He was dressed in lounge clothes, black sweatpants and a loose t-shirt with a graphic from an animated show he liked, and that he knew Fen liked as well. The green streak of hair he had dyed not long ago was still vibrant, though the color hadn't turned out quite right. He shook his head, attempting to clear his thoughts. He shoved his phone back in his pants pocket as he undid the lock and turned the handle of the door.

There stood Fen, a beaming ray of sunlight that made him remember what the daytime looked like. His eyeliner was smokey, making his gaze up into Soren's face all the more beautiful. His breath caught, and he felt himself staring but couldn't help it. He resisted the temptation to tuck a strand of Fen's sleek black hair back, wondering what it would feel like. The moments felt stretched inside his chest, pulling until taut, his resolve slipping. Soren had to do something else, anything else besides look into Fen's eyes.

"Um," Fen said, looking away shyly. "Can I come in?"

Soren's composure returned, albeit in a weakened state. He cleared his throat, rubbing the back of his neck with one hand and pulling the door open wide with the other. "Yeah, yeah come on in."

"Thanks!"

As Fen stepped inside and Soren shut the door, he turned his head left and right, surveying the new area. Soren felt suddenly self-conscious, and he shook his head as if to physically push the feeling away. He had no reason to be so disquieted; Fen was not going to judge his apartment. At least, he hoped not.

"So," he started, keeping his hands firmly in his pockets and keeping a rather awkward distance from Fen. "Can I get you anything?"

He shook his head, turning to face Soren with an approving look. "This is a cute place! You cleaned it before I came, I'll bet."

He was teasing him. That was a good sign, and it made Soren feel more comfortable. "I might not live in a Royal house, but I like to think it's still nice."

Fen began to step towards him, and Soren's breath stopped, but he ended up staying in his place.

Come closer, he thought, though did not say.

"You don't need to get me anything right now, but thank you for offering," Fen said, his gaze off to the side, avoiding eye contact. "Where should I sit, though?"

They had been standing there since Fen came in, and Soren silently cursed himself for being so stiff. He had snuck into Fen's room multiple times to talk and play games for hours, why was this so different?

"Sorry, yeah, the couch is over there, we can sit."

They both strode over to the plush gray couch in front of a TV that had been playing soft music in the background to fill the empty space. As Soren sat on his usual side, he looked at Fen and watched the gears turn in his pretty little head, and he figured he was working out where he should sit. He could take a place on the opposite side, leaving a seat open between them, or he could take the closest spot. As his face reddened, Soren felt a fondness in his heart that made him disregard any nerves from before. This was Fen, he had nothing to worry about.

He patted the spot right next to him, crossing his legs and leaning his chin in one hand as his elbow sat on the arm of the couch. "Sit here," he urged.

Relief flooded Fen's face and he promptly sat down, though he seemed a bit rigid.

The heat from his body directly next to Soren was evident and dizzying, and he realized he wanted Fen to be closer. He wanted them to touch. He wanted to touch him. Uncrossing his legs, he let his knee bump into Fen's. That was all he could allow himself for the time being. It was clear enough to him that Fen at least felt something towards him, but he had no idea to what level. It was becoming obvious to Soren that his own level was only rising. The weeks of them talking and flirting hadn't culminated into anything physical yet, and though he wanted it, he did not want to rush the other vampire. He cared for him too much to ruin what they already had. As he thought to himself, he sighed, and Fen raised his eyebrows at him.

"What is it?" he asked Soren.

Asking Fen to join him on the mission had to be first. Before anything else, he needed to come clean and let him know his plans, or else the dread of it would haunt him the whole night. A part of him was excited, and the other part worried. He assured himself for what seemed like the hundredth time that no matter what, he would keep Fen safe if anything went wrong.

"I have something to ask you," he started. "I want to get it out of the way first, just so I'm not stuck thinking about it the whole time you're here."

"Soren," he said, his name on his tongue like a high he wanted to feel for hours. "Just ask, you'll just make me nervous the more you stall."

Out with it. "There's a mission I'm going on for the Rogues tomorrow night. It's supposed to be a really important one, but I don't know all the details yet. They don't want to give it all away. I guess in case of any leaks. There are five other vampires going, and I thought maybe you'd like to join. Only if you want to, of course."

"Yes," Fen said instantly.

He should have known he would agree without asking, without thinking about it for more than a second. It was a horrible feeling, wanting so badly for him to go, and yet wishing he would stay home. He felt like he was turning into Lorcan, their protective attitude rubbing off on him. It made him realize that it ultimately wasn't his choice, and that Fen deserved to make his own decisions. He would not take that away from him, even if at times he wanted to, if only to make sure he stayed alive, and stayed exactly the way he was.

"Are you sure?" he asked, his tone serious. "This isn't like when I went to the ball. This is dangerous, I'm positive, or else they wouldn't send this many of us. I just want you to know what you're agreeing to, even though what I know myself is limited."

Fen's face was hard set as he stared at the ground, fists clenched in his lap. "Yes, I'm sure. I haven't been able to help until now, and I want the chance to."

His face turned to him, and his expression became so sincere it made Soren's eyes widen involuntarily.

"Thank you for asking me to go," he said, smiling. "Thank you for... trusting me, I guess."

Soren realized at that moment he would do anything for him—this boy with emerald eyes and a soft face, emotions that were as clear as a full moon, and a determination to help others that always outweighed his own logic. He would let him do anything he wanted, and he would help him do it. Wanting so, so badly to touch Fen, he used every ounce of strength he had to keep still. It was maddening.

"Of course," he said, returning Fen's smile, genuinely. "I'll be there with you the whole time, so if you need me I won't be far."

Fen nodded, his hands now playing with the hem of his baggy shirt that showed too much of his collarbone and certainly did not make Soren restless. "I know your Blessing is more offensive, but mine is more… defensive, you could say. I don't want to just rely on you to protect me the whole time, but I'd be lying if I said I was a master at any combat."

While Soren had told Fen about his Blessing and even showed him some party tricks with it, he still did not know what Fen's was. It was clear the thought of it held uncomfortable memories that he didn't want to press on, so him mentioning it now was more of a hint than he had ever gotten. Still, he did not want to push, so he nodded in understanding.

"I get it, there's plenty of silver weapons we have saved up. I even have some here, if you want to borrow anything, whatever would make you feel more comfortable."

Fen's brows knitted together, a pained expression clouding his beautiful features. "Huh, weapons. I guess... yeah, that makes sense. If I'm being honest, I'd rather have that as a last resort, but I get that things might not be smooth."

It was clear to Soren that Fen did not like the idea of hurting anyone, or really anything. He was so sweet, and Soren's chest tightened. "Just as a last resort, then. It doesn't hurt to be prepared, just in case."

"Just in case," he agreed.

The mood was beginning to sour, and Soren had to do something fast before it furthered. He would be damned if this night was ruined, he had been looking forward to it and he would enjoy his time with Fen if he could control it.

"So," he said, relaxing his body and shifting his tone to be more playful. "Now that you're here, what do you want to do?"

"Oh!" Fen perked up, reaching for a shoulder bag Soren hadn't noticed him having when he came in. "I brought some of the games we talked about, the ones you wanted to try!"

He pulled out multiple video games and displayed them to Soren, which made his shirt shift over to one side, almost revealing his whole shoulder, his bare skin pale and perfect. He enjoyed the view for a moment before responding. "I just wanted to borrow them, they're not multiplayer."

Fen's cheeks flushed, eyes darting around nervously. "I thought I could watch you play for a while. I'd be happy with that."

Soren, seemingly not paying full attention to his own body, leaned his leg more into Fen's, going from brushing knees to pressed legs. His skin tingled, warm where they touched. He did not move. "You pick," he said, daring to stare into Fen's face, tracing every detail into memory.

"O-Okay, this one then?" he asked, voice shaky and hands trembling slightly as he held the game out to Soren.

He wanted to touch Fen more. He felt like he had to, like the weeks gone by with only brushes and words and glances had only tided him over until that moment. Fen was there, his skin, his breath, his leg touching his, and it made his mind falter again and again. It wasn't enough, he needed more and he needed it soon. His hands drifted towards Fen, taking all the games from him and placing them on the side table next to the couch, all the while never breaking eye contact as Fen's gaze fixated on him.

When the games were out of the way, his hand went back, and he laced his fingers with Fen's, holding their hands together in front of them.

It felt like kindling being swallowed by flames, spreading from his fingertips throughout his whole hand, the contact fevering his thoughts. It was so simple, and it made him insane. Watching Fen's face turn red, his breath quickening, Soren no longer cared about the Rogues, the mission, or his own hatred of the Royals. The only thing on his mind was the vampire in front of him, and how badly he wanted him. Should he ask if Fen felt the same? Would he need him this desperately? What if he didn't? The thought struck fear into his core, the idea scaring him more than death itself.

Soren began to lean forward, eyes hazy, focusing only on Fen's face, his breathing, his lips. He stopped short of his destination, closing his eyes as he whispered, "Can I?"

Fen's hand gripped Soren's tighter as he inhaled sharply. "Yes," he said, breathless, wanting.

And he kissed him, closing the distance between their lips as his whole world felt as if it had shifted. All thoughts, all emotions, and all logic fled, leaving only Fen's skin. His free hand gripped the back of Fen's neck, pulling him closer and kissing him harder, his mouth opening slightly, tongue against the other man's lips. Fen made a small sound, and it sent Soren spinning. This hunger was unlike anything he had felt before, in either of his lives, human or vampire. His desire bloomed in his whole body, feeling Fen's tongue against his own. In a moment, his hand that had been holding Fen's let go, and instead wrapped around his back, pulling their chests together as he leaned him downwards to lie on the couch. Soren's body pressed against Fen's, their kisses rough, desperate, starving. He was on top of Fen, one hand still keeping a firm grip on his neck, the other cautiously moving towards the bottom of Fen's shirt.

He pulled up the fabric, Fen's bare chest exposed as his sounds only became more frequent. Nothing else was around them, he was convinced. The only two beings in the world were right there, his hand had never felt anything better than Fen's bare skin as he caressed him, then went to grab his hip firmly. Fen's breath hitched, his hands jerking upwards to Soren's back, gripping his shirt in his hands, urging his body closer.

He was everything. He was his obsession, all he wanted and more. Fen's voice was soft and breathless, his skin hot to the touch and smooth, and his body was so close—painfully, agonizingly close. As they broke their mouths apart only to shed their shirts, he could not admit the overwhelming feeling his mind formulated. He could not say the words. Fen broke their kiss for a horrifying moment, and Soren heard a whispered voice in his ear, obsidian hair tickling his cheek.

"Bed," he said simply, shivering. "Please."

He did not reply, instead he lifted Fen up, his legs wrapping around Soren's torso, arms around his neck, head leaning against his shoulder. He carried him across the room to the bed, laying him down gently, and he was able to see for the first time. He gazed at Fen's shirtless body, and though he never thought Fen was the tattoo type, there it was: a Chinese-style dragon, all in red ink, spanning up Fen's right side and disappearing into his pants. As Fen met his gaze, skin flushed and eyes half-lidded with lust, not being able to see the rest of the tattoo pushed him into near madness. He needed him. In every way that he could have him, he needed him. It was terrifying, realizing just how deep he had gotten himself.

"Soren," Fen said, and his voice was like the most glorious song he had ever heard. "Kiss me."

Soren would've killed for him if he had asked. Anything Fen would ask of him, any wish, he would grant it. He would at least start with the kiss.

Chapter 11

Fen

Fen awoke to the sound of a door closing and a sink running, a sliver of light breaching beneath the bathroom door. He blinked the sleep from his eyes, turning on his side and watching the shadows of Soren's footsteps from the bed. Reaching for his phone behind him on the bedside table, he checked the time. They had hours still until the night, until the inevitable event that he knew would change something. A knot in his stomach wound tighter. Fen did not know what the change would be, or just how large, but he knew it was coming.

The door squeaked open, slowly and gently. Soren walked out with no shirt and messy hair, bathed in the darkness of the apartment. Fen had to stare. He did not regret being with Soren; it was quite the opposite. He wanted for nothing else, but fear was etched behind his eyes, and Soren, stepping closer with a soft look of concern, somehow knew. It was both comforting and infuriating, the way he could decipher what was on Fen's face so quickly. He was never good at hiding his emotions, but Soren saw them in their rawest form. It was terrifying.

"What is it?" Soren asked as he slipped back into bed, lying on his side to bring his face toward Fen's.

The Prince bit his lip, looking at the pillow below the Rogue's head instead of his eyes. "Nerves, mostly."

Soren's brows knitted and he rested his hand on top of Fen's. "Tell me."

He sighed, lacing his fingers with Soren's. Fen did not want him to think he was scared and meek, a Prince in distress. But he was, in a way. He feared having a silver weapon in his hands, ending a life he did not know the impact of. Would it be someone's sister? Brother? Someone who meant to another what Soren meant to him? He thought for a moment about what that might be. What was Soren to him? What was he to Soren? It ate at him with everything else on his mind, the feeling tying the knot tighter.

"I don't want you to think badly of me," Fen finally said.

"What do you mean?" Soren's tone was so full of fondness it made his throat dry. "I don't think at this point you could do anything like that."

"What if I did?" Fen asked, feeling his eyes turn dewy. "I want to come and I will, but I don't want to kill. I'm scared of that, scared of who it might make me. I'm..."

Soren's eyes bore into him, making Fen squirm. He spoke too much, it was impossible to go back.

"I'm afraid of what I might do for you."

Soren's hand squeezed his, and he pressed his forehead to Fen's. They both closed their eyes, breaths soft and careful.

"I fear the same. I hope you don't change your mind about me once you see what we do. The Rogues have a reason, a damn good one, but our methods aren't moral. We kill because we have to. I don't want you to regret being with me because of it."

Fen knew vampires, and he knew for years that they think of death differently than him. He could never change his mind, no matter how many years passed. Fen never had to kill, and if he could help it, he never would.

"I don't think I could," Fen whispered. "I can't regret you."

-

The handle of the silver dagger in Fen's hands was cold and heavy, the glint of the blade seeming to tempt him. It promised blood and finality. He sheathed it quickly on his thigh and turned his attention to Lorcan. They were typing away on a laptop, screen bright with a million things that Fen didn't need to know. Soren was just behind him, slipping a sword into a sheath at his back. He said he did not need a weapon, that his Blessing was more than enough, but Fen had insisted. The Prince looked around the room of Rogues and counted. Four vampires he knew nothing about were strapping weapons onto themselves and speaking in hushed tones of anticipation. Their auras were electric, a static passing through the room that spoke of their excitement. Whenever they felt Fen's eyes on them, they glowered. They did not trust Fen fully, though Soren had advocated for him many times, but they seemed to like Lorcan just fine.

It was no different than a ball. Vampires gathered for a purpose he could not fully understand, whispering in what seemed like a foreign language. For them, blood was not only a thirst, but a hunger. They killed and would again and again. Fen let himself slip away from their pull, focusing ahead of him and ignoring all he could. Loran handed him an earpiece that he slipped on wordlessly, his friend serious and commanding. It was odd to see them like that instead of how they were in the castle. Lorcan was usually so mischievous and light, bouncing from vampire to vampire and event to event. They were loud and always kept the spotlight, but here, they were background noise.

A hand on his shoulder snapped Fen out of his thoughts. Soren was next to him all in black. A long-sleeve compression shirt hugged his body in a way that Fen had to tear his eyes from and instead glanced at leather boots and slightly baggy pants with several pockets. Soren already had his earpiece on, his other tattooed hand fiddling with it in annoyance. He looked exactly the part of the handsome Rogue itching for a fight and it made Fen wonder just how badly he stuck out in comparison. He wore a black t-shirt and athletic sweatpants he had to borrow from Soren, though he had his own black and white sneakers. He felt exposed without his usual necklaces and rings, the only accessory the dagger strapped to his thigh. It was all so painfully not Fen.

"Are you okay?" Soren whispered into Fen's ear.

He nodded, a response cut off by Lorcan instructing them all to test their equipment, ensuring they could be heard by everyone.

Lorcan was to stay in the weapons room with their laptop, keeping a constant vigilance for intel from the Rogues. They would all leave by two different cars, the directions to their destination already inputted into GPS inside. Soren, Fen, and a vampire named Trinity would go in one car, the rest of the Rogues in the other. Soren insisted on driving; he and Trinity had playfully argued over it as they adjourned and made their way into the parking garage. Fen stayed silent, nodding along to instructions and toying with the handle of the dagger, picking at it with his black nails, the polish beginning to chip.

In the end, Soren had lost a game of rock paper scissors with Trinity by the time Fen was slipping into the back seat. Soren jumped in next to him, buckling his seatbelt and setting his sword upright next to him, all while his eyes never left Fen. It made him blush, his cheeks warming before reaching his hand to Soren's, gripping it with more force than he meant to. The worry was clear on his face as Fen lessened his grip. He mouthed silently to Fen as the car started and Trinity began to follow the GPS screen glowing in the front.

Are you okay?

Fen nodded, but pulled out his phone and typed into his notes, turning the screen to Soren.

Just nervous, that's all :)

Soren swiped the phone from Fen, typing and then handing it back.

You sure?

He nodded again, squeezing Soren's hand in comfort this time.

Fen's anxiety eased a bit as Soren squeezed back, a delicate smile on his sharp, beautiful face. Fen needed to know what was waiting for them, no matter how he feared everything changing. He had to know what was happening to the missing Rogues, and if the Royals truly were behind it. He had to know if vampires were dying.

He would know soon enough.

-

As Trinity pulled the car into a vacant dirt lot, Fen heard Lorcan's voice in his earpiece. "Just saw you guys pull up. How is it looking?"

Trinity answered, her voice high and lovely, though her tone was serious. "The others got here first. Looks like they're checking the outside, but it's quiet out here."

"Good," Lorcan said, and Fen could imagine the small nod of their head. "It's what's inside that we need, get in once the coast is clear."

A ways out from their parking spot was a huge gray building, all concrete and square with no windows, not a single soul in sight save for the Rogues. It looked to Fen like a box, one meant to keep things inside. Escape was only a word, never a possibility. His nerves surged like a tide in the moonlit night as he watched Soren and Trinity grab their weapons and open the car doors, Soren pulling Fen to exit on his side. He wasn't sure if he had the strength to let go of Soren's hand and hoped it wouldn't show.

"It's clear," Soren said after the other vampires in the distance gave the signal.

The three of them made their way to the looming fortress, its angles cold and unyielding in the dark. It was the loneliest building Fen had ever seen.

The Prince's nervous hand went to the handle of the dagger again, picking at it as they walked. He hoped he wouldn't have to use it; he willed it with all his might. Fear came in many forms and his head spun in an attempt to keep up with it all. While the area seemed all but abandoned, he knew better. Whatever was inside the depressing fortress was somehow worth risking lives to the Rogues, and some small sliver of hopefulness clung to the back of his mind. This could be where the missing vampires were being held; they could save them all tonight and be done with it. Soren and Fen could move on and figure out where they were headed, and he hoped it would be together.

The group of vampires halted at what seemed to be the only door, a large rectangle of black metal with a keypad meant for a code. Fen could hear Lorcan in his earpiece, the sound of laptop keys and hushed curses coming at a steady pace until a *click* sounded from the keypad. Fen had questions, so very many, but his mouth would not open to ask them. He would wait, and he would get answers soon enough.

Soren eagerly took the lead, one hand poised on the door handle, the other holding a finger to his lips as his eyes scanned the group. His gaze rested on Fen, the sudden and firm eye contact sending a static shock to Fen's spine. Soren was making sure he was ready, and he let that gesture bring a glimmer of comfort, keeping it close in his short supply. He gave a curt nod, and Soren turned back to the door.

The change was instantaneous, the very air around Soren rising in temperature as he swiftly opened the door, his free hand alighting in a contained fire. He held it in front of him, casting light into the dark interior of the building. Fen had only seen Soren perform a few small sparks and flames before, and he had thought them delicate and lovely. Now, he knew better. Just the one fire in his hands felt like a pull, a power that could only build and never wane. Soren was like the edge of a cliffside, one step away from a plummet into something wild. It was no wonder the Rogues kept him for missions; he could be power itself if he chose to be.

They all fell in line one by one, following Soren inside as they let his fire guide them. Lorcan had instructed them that while cameras were disabled in the building, security guards would still be lurking in the halls. They had to be armed and confident, Fen thought, as the sterile tile floors gave away any steps, smooth white walls echoing the sounds further. They all were as quiet as possible, slow and deliberate, save for Soren. While he made sure to keep stealthy, his posture was tall and cocky. He did not think anyone could beat him, and Fen believed it.

The halls were void, with no doors or windows. The ceilings held cameras sporadically that all were lifeless for the time being. The building was a maze of white with no lights, seemingly endless corridors with no purpose. It made the back of Fen's neck prickle, sweat accumulating every time Soren rounded a corner. What was the building for? Was it empty as a decoy? Was it all one large trap? The possibilities seethed in his mind, and every moment passing stretched into more paranoia. Something was going to happen, and they all knew it, the air between them all taut. No one dared speak, hands resting on weapons in protection. It was agonizing.

The moment Soren rounded another corner and let out a soft gasp, they all tensed and halted in fear. Fen was a few vampires behind, and he could not see the Rogue. His body nearly ached with the urge to go to him, the want to shield the Rogue swelling. He heard a horribly loud door squeaking open and winced, gripping the dagger at his thigh so hard his nails bent. His foot slid forward an inch, eyes trained at the corner of the hall. No one was moving, all of them statues frozen on their feet.

The flame from Soren's hand popped from the corner, his face following and illuminated in warmth.

"Found it," he said, jerking his head to his side.

They all began to breathe again, though still carefully. Fen's grip loosened, fingers still near enough just in case.

Once Fen saw where they were going, he understood Soren's reaction.

It was a dead-end hallway, the only door they found in the expanse of halls was in the floor, a basement illuminated by fluorescent lights akin to a hospital. There were concrete stairs leading down into matching white walls and flooring, but Fen could just make out what looked like glass observation windows, and more black metal doors with keypads. The vampires began their descent, Soren holding the door open for them all as he kept watch. Once he saw Fen, he reached out a hand to rest on his, the one still touching the dagger.

"Wait for me down there," he whispered, his tone a mix of command and worry.

All Fen could do was nod before the sound of a blade being drawn echoed up to his ears. Soren held an arm in front of Fen's chest, pushing him a step back as he leapt down into the door, the weight of it slamming down behind him.

Chapter 12

Fen

Violence erupted so loudly Fen's ears rang, his hands frantically grasping to reopen the door. Trinity was there next to him, her hands far more steady as she successfully pulled it open, revealing the scene below.

Soren and two of the other Rogues were in a dance of silver and blood with black-clad vampires all in medical garb, though their weapons made it clear they were not innocent medical personnel. Five were in sight, two of them already lying on the floor in pools, and a third was beginning to bloom into a flower of sunset and ash, licks of fire-like petals unfurling along flesh. Soren's hands snaked with long flames going up his arms, crossing together almost like whips, the lick of them igniting his foes.

It was a scene Fen had imagined, but could not fathom now that it was playing before him. Soren alight just as his flames were, his dark hair glowing and his skin golden. He was Apollo, standing before mortals in light and splendor and carnage. Every move he made was flowing and skilled, his body

117

a vision in red and yellow and orange. He was awe-inspiring as a forest fire, snuffing out all in his path with a mercy nature did not know. It intoxicated Fen, the display of strength an entirely new side of Soren he could not look away from. He was not afraid of Soren, he only feared what may happen if the power he watched in awe were to burn out. The Prince would not allow it.

Trinity, Fen, and the remaining Rogues all made their way down, joining in the fray. Fen stayed back, watching for signs of others who may follow the commotion. Disconcertingly, none came. The enemy vampires were all dead on the ground, Trinity swiping a keycard from one of the fallen. Soren's fire dissipated, leaving only the smell of charred bodies and smoke. He immediately found Fen and he strode over to him with purpose. Though he did not touch him, his face was tender enough to make up for it. It struck Fen just how different this Rogue was around him. His godlike fury was gone, the remnants at their feet, and here he was with the expression of a docile lover moments after. He realized then that Soren would do anything for him. He would become Apollo again; he had something waiting for him when the battle was won.

Fen wanted that. He craved freedom and yearned for an end with his flame, one where it need not burn so viciously.

Once they all had a moment to regain composure and wait for any reinforcements, weapons were sheathed and voices picked up. Trinity was speaking to Lorcan in her earpiece, telling them about the basement and the vampires in black scrubs and lab coats. It all faded into the background for Fen, his eyes distant and unfocused. He looked past Soren at one of the black doors, peering past it as he tried to see inside the large glass window beside it. Fen began to walk forward, pulling Soren along by the hand, his grip firmer than he meant it to be. Neither of them spoke as they neared the unknown rooms, the picture inside them coming into focus.

Four vampires were detained upright into stands, thick silver bands holding them down at every point across their bodies. They all had straps across their mouths and eyes, keeping them blind and mute. Their heads were all limp, none of them conscious. Clear tubes were attached to all of their necks, weaving upwards and then down into a vat. Only one seemed to be turned on, a leisurely stream of blood being sucked from their neck through the tube and deposited into its destination. Fen turned around, slowly, numbly. The second room was identical, down to the number of captive vampires. He could hear Soren speaking, his voice muffled and distant while Fen's mind reeled. How many were down there?

The Prince turned again, walking back to the dead on the floor, fingertips and toes tingling. He felt a sickness in him, a dread he had only known once before. There was nothing but pain here, everything awash in bright white lights and the steady breaths of prisoners. At that moment, he did not care what he had to do; the trapped must be freed. Soren was tugging at his hand, urging him to stop, to speak, to look at him. He could not. All he could do was bend down and grab an access card, wetness brushing his fingers and staining them red. He walked back to the door, reaching towards the keypad, about to swipe it over the sensor.

A pale, lovely hand met his, covering the card and smearing blood. Soren was in front of him, looking down into his face in a twisted expression of concern. Fen's stomach dropped, seeing him like that. He was being impulsive, he wasn't thinking, he wasn't aware. His knees shook, threatening to give way. Trinity's voice went louder, coming closer.

"The fuck is he doing?" she snapped, glaring at Soren.

The expression of concern on Soren's face peeled away, and pure, dizzying anger raced over his eyes at Trinity. Fen's head went foggy, seeing the amber eyes of his flame go dark.

"Leave him be," Soren growled.

There was no room to object. He was flint, begging to be struck. Trinity knew better, and she huffed, walking past them deeper into the hallway.

He looked back to Fen, face changing again, and Fen was drunk on everything around him. The feeling was like being underwater, submerged in a lake with muck clouding his view. He willed himself to snap out of it, to be stronger, to not let the lights that reminded him so much of the hospital from twenty-five years ago send him into a panic. His whole body felt far away, so faded and sad. A woman's face flashed in his memory and he almost let out a cry. He should never have come along.

Soren carefully, so carefully, like he was handling a wounded butterfly, rested his grip on Fen's shoulders. His body came closer to where they were almost pressed together, and he rested his chin on the top of Fen's head. His warm breath, steady hands, and strong presence were enough to give Fen just enough bravery. It was embarrassing, just how weak he felt, how this place was disarming him in a way he did not think possible. His memories were being pushed back so far he feared they would tear a hole in his skull. But still, he pressed on, and he persevered. He had to.

"We have to get them out," Fen pleaded, his voice hoarse and small. "Please."

"Of course," Soren said, rubbing his hands up and down Fen's upper arms. "We will. I promise."

"Now," he begged, desperate. "I don't know how much longer I can be here. The lights, the smells, the fucking walls, I can't stand it here."

Soren did not press, did not ask why. He did not need to know, he only knew Fen was unhappy and that was all it took.

The other Rogues' voices made their way to his ears, their voices becoming clearer. Trinity was farthest, her voice echoing down more white hallways. Fen wondered if this place was endless, and he feared staying and finding out.

"There are labs down here," one Rogue said. "Fancy equipment for who knows what."

"Take pictures, send them to Lorcan, I'm sure they'll know more about it."

"Got it."

Only footsteps and silence followed, and it made Fen burn inside. No one was opening the doors. The kidnapped vampires were there, helpless, and no one was helping them. A rage began to build in his chest, his grip on the keycard becoming so tight the plastic cut into his fingers, stinging and waking him up further. Soren felt it, and he tried to gently pull the card away from Fen. He would not let go. He had to do something. If no one else would, it had to be him.

"Oh fuck," a Rogue said, popping around the corner after a moment, their face grim. "There's a storage room. It's got rows and rows of some kind of potion. Like, a million of them."

Trinity strode to them, keycard in hand. "Show me."

Fen didn't care about some fucking potion. He cared about the vampires being drained against their will, kept like animals, drugged and comatose. If the Rogues could do whatever they wanted, he would do the same.

"We should check it out," Soren said, soft, so soft, and Fen nearly faltered.

Fen shook his head. "We need to get these vampires out. Now. Please, help me."

He sighed, pushing Fen away a few inches to make eye contact. "We need to find out what's going on first. We don't know when more of these fucked up vampires might come. There are only so many of us, so if we make a better plan later we can get them all out. Right now, we could only manage a few."

"So we're just going to leave them?" Fen asked, incredulous.

"No, we can still get some of them, but we don't have the numbers to get them all. Fen, please," he tried taking the keycard again, and the last of Fen's calmness snapped.

"No, we get them *now*."

At that moment, three things happened at once.

There was the sound of a door opening down the hallway, the Rogues gathering some of the potions to take back with them, their voices confident and upbeat, distracted.

The door up the stairs, the only exit they knew, opened up to reveal vampires in heavy black gear, helmets covering their faces, and weapons in their hands.

The shrill *beep* of the door in front of Fen opened as he swiped his keycard, so fast Soren didn't have the time to react.

As Fen pushed the door open, a *click* just inside of it sounded, and Soren's eyes widened in horror.

He did not know why, he did not know anything. The boots of the vampires pounded down the stairs, the Rogues ran to face them, and before Fen could enter the room to save the trapped individuals, Soren pushed him backwards so hard he fell, landing on the cold floor. He had been facing the door, pushing it open behind Soren, trying to step around him to enter the room, and with the force of the push, Soren staggered inside. A panel on the ceiling opened, and a palm-sized silver orb toppled onto the floor. Fen could only see Soren through the observation window, his stomach dropping instantly. Everything was happening too fast, and he was scared, so scared.

He watched. Everything slowed, the sounds of fighting behind him, Soren turning to meet his eyes through the glass. The cloud of glittering silver smoke began to fill the room. He knew then, he knew too late. Tears welled in his eyes, his body not moving fast enough. Soren was holding the door shut while Fen panicked, all his strength to push on the door, his shaking limbs barely keeping him upright. The door would not open.

He watched. The silver smoke was crawling up the walls, into the open space. It reached the captive vampires, and they seized. Their bodies spasmed, blood dripping out from behind their covered mouths and eyes, noses a waterfall of crimson. They were asleep, and then they were dead. The smoke was filling the entire room, and Soren's sad smile would be ingrained within Fen's mind for the rest of his second life.

He watched. Soren's hands slipped from the door handle, limp. His smile faded, replaced with rolled-back eyes and blood. His body fell to the floor, and Fen could not see him anymore. Tears cascaded down his face, and he felt a horrible, strained cry escape his lips.

He had been stupid. He had not stopped to think of traps. He had not stopped to think at all.

The silver bomb was an invention rarely used, and he had only heard about them from Lorcan once when they had been in a vampire research phase. All kinds of silver weapons were made by vampires to kill each other; no other material worked as well. The bombs were the hardest to control. They released a smoke with fine silver that filled the air, death imminent the moment a vampire breathed it in. Fen never thought he would need to know. He had half listened to Lorcan, believing there would never be a time the weapon would threaten his life.

He had been wrong.

He heard Trinity yelling over the commotion, all of the Rogues engrossed in combat. He did not hear her the first time, only once she was gripping the front of his shirt, her face hot and angry just inches from his.

"We have to *go*," she spat. "Unless you feel like dying here."

He couldn't. And he would not.

"Hold them off," he said simply.

Her eyes went wide, shocked at his gall. "What?"

"Keep them away from me. I won't take long."

126

He pulled her wrist away from him, replacing her hand upon his shirt with his own, pulling the fabric over his mouth and nose.

The smoke in the room was dissipating, fading into nothing, leaving only its victims as evidence. He had to be quick, just in case any might escape. It was worth the risk.

Fen swiped the keycard for the second time, opening the door and flinging his hand inside, finding Soren's wrist, and he pulled. He heaved Soren's body out of the room, slamming the door shut just as fast in his wake.

He had sworn never to do this again. He had promised only one person that he would do this, and he made the oath to himself. Never again. Not since Mother.

He would have to come to terms with his broken promise another time.

He laid Soren on his back, resting his arms beside his lifeless body. Fen tried not to look at his bloodied face, his sobs just barely being held back. His hands rested on top of each other, pressed against Soren's chest that did not move. The electric tingle of power he had felt many years ago edged along his body, filling all his senses. He became static and light, his vision blinded by the glow of his hands. He pulled, and he pushed. There was no way to explain how his Blessing worked, only that he knew it like his own mind. Practice did not matter, he knew.

His eyes flooded and overflowed, his tears landing on his hands and Soren's chest, warm and damp, disappearing into the light.

He said only one word, and it came out like a thousand different voices, in a thousand different times, in a million wishes of the same thing.

"Follow."

Chapter 13

Soren

Nothing.

Empty inside.

Desolate and cold.

Everything was nothing and then there was something. There was a light, maybe. He could not tell. Nothing felt like anything, it was dark. But there was a light, he thought. How could he catch it? Like a firefly blinking in and out of view, the light was there, he was sure.

There was a sound. He knew there was. It was loud, booming, the most terrifying thing he had ever heard. He could not resist it. He dared not.

"Follow."

Chapter 14

Soren

Soren awoke in a frenzied cough and to the firm grip of someone pulling to make him sit up. He blinked and blinked, the bright light he had seen just beginning to fade as he regained his vision. He felt awful and he felt marvelous. He tried to remember, the memories coming back so slowly he feared they would slip away in the wait. A voice he knew, one that made his heart flutter and his body ache, became clear.

"Soren?" it asked, his name sounding like fresh honey on a summer day.

He coughed again, his throat clearing, his breaths steady, his vision back. He was still disoriented, but he managed to lift his head.

Fen was there, with his lovely green eyes and his soft pretty face and his silky black hair. Was he real? Was Soren dreaming somehow? What had they been doing?

"Soren," Fen said again. "How do you feel?"

He reached up and brushed Fen's cheek, and a panic rose when he pulled away and left a red stain where his hand had been.

"What happened?" Soren asked.

Fen looked like he was going to vomit, his face drained of color and his skin clammy.

"What happened?" he asked again.

The sounds of a battle suddenly reached Soren, and he rose to stand.

His legs were strong, so strong it made him gasp. He felt *good.*

He heaved Fen up by his hand, steadying the Prince against his shoulder.

"Fen," he urged for the third time, "What happened?"

There wasn't time to elaborate as Trinity bounded over to them, a look of pure shock and awe written on her face. She would not stop staring at Fen.

"We held them off," she said. "That won't be the last of them. We need to go and we won't wait around this time."

Fen nodded, but forlornly looked into the room beside them. There were four vampires strapped upwards, all of them streaked with blood from their eyes, noses, and mouths.

"Okay," he agreed.

Soren slept the entire ride back to the city, the soothing strokes of Fen's hand on his upper arm lulling him into slumber. He had a vague dream, nothing but blinking light and tears, until the tickle of his hair being brushed from his forehead woke him. Fen was there; his skin was pale, strikingly pale, not like him at all. It worried him more than anything else. The gap in his memory would not fill, though he strained until an ache formed in his head. He just wanted Fen to be okay, to be back to his blushing, happy self. Anything was worth that.

Soren, Fen, and Trinity exited the car and left it in the same parking garage they had taken it from, all of them silent and tense. He wanted to ask for details again, to figure out why they were all so damn quiet. It frustrated him enough to put his mood even more on edge. Was this what Fen felt like normally? Out of the loop, secrets just an everyday occurrence he was never privy to? He could see why he hated it so much.

They all made their way to Lorcan's low-lit tech room, the air inside just as tense but with a touch of frenzy. Lorcan was clearing space on a large table, letting the Rogues set down what they had taken from the oppressive concrete building they so

132

narrowly escaped. Soren had not counted the bodies of the dead, though he did see two were burnt—his work, he presumed. There had been many, and it was a wonder they all had made it back alive. It only made him all the more puzzled. His memories were in bits and pieces, dark hallways turned to stark overhead lights, his fire catching on bodies, the four dead captives, and Fen crying over him. Everything was hazy and he wanted so badly for it to clear. He figured it was only a matter of time as the Rogues spread out the mission's spoils.

They all placed vials upon vials of black liquid in corked glass bottles down on the table. None had labels; they were all identical and mysterious. One of them set down a bloodied plastic card, and another a stack of crinkled, nearly ruined papers. Soren was stuck on the bottles, their contents unlike anything he had ever seen.

He looked to his side, and there was Fen. Soren went to hold his hand in comfort, and when their skin touched, he winced. Fen's hand was sweaty, cold, and trembling. *What the fuck happened?*

Lorcan took a wide-eyed look at the items on the table, slowly reaching towards the stack of papers. Their eyes flicked to Fen so fast Soren almost missed it, their expression unreadable.

They began to flip through them, trying not to touch too much of the blood and dirt staining the stack, eyes scanning the words. Everyone waited, barely able to breathe. Then, Lorcan stopped, set down the papers, and instead reached for one of the vials. They peered into the liquid, disbelieving and fearful. Their lips pursed, face turning grave as they faced the group.

"What happened?" they asked.

That's what Soren wanted to know. The gaps in his memory were becoming more worrisome by the minute.

Trinity stepped forward, shooting a look over to Fen, almost like she was asking him for permission. Fen did nothing but stare at the floor and grip Soren's hand tighter.

It was clear Lorcan was trying not to show bias towards Fen, but they still stole a glance at him, a look of sadness in their eyes.

They turned back to Trinity. "Go on," they said.

And Trinity began telling a tale that made Soren feel far away from his body. She spoke of the vampires strapped with silver across their bodies, blood being harvested from their necks. The rooms of lab equipment and files upon files of research, and finally, the room full of vials. So many that they had not bothered counting, and then she went quiet. Just for one painful moment, until her words seemed foreign.

She said Soren died. She said a silver bomb had gone off, and he ended up in the room. He had inhaled the smoke, and he had died.

Then she said Fen brought him back.

Soren stood so still he thought he may never move again.

At the last bit, Lorcan's face went rigid and they could not hide it. Though they said nothing directly to Soren, he knew the look was for him.

"I know this is going to sound odd," they said to everyone, "but we need to ignore that for now."

Trinity became heated, her tone snapping. "Ignore the fact that this *Prince* can bring people back from the dead? That's not something we can just brush away, Lorcan. Do you know what he could do with that? We could do *anything*."

"I don't care right now," Lorcan said, rubbing their eyes in frustration. "Did any of you read these files?"

The Rogues shook their heads.

"These vials," Lorcan began, picking the papers back up. "I don't think you could even guess how fucked we are. Every Rogue alive is not only going to be left behind, but probably used for blood harvesting, if you're unlucky. Dead at best."

They paused to sigh, sitting down and leaning back in their chair, clearly exhausted. Soren just wanted them to spit it out.

"These are currently being called Sun Potions. Any guesses on what they do?"

The wheels in Soren's mind began to turn, an itching feeling of dread building.

"From what the papers claim, these will let vampires walk in the sun. As long as someone has the right connections, they could cease to have the one real weakness we all have. The papers don't say this, but let's be honest here. The Royals are planning to use these to make the world theirs, because nothing would stop them. They will control the supply and demand and make sure only the ones they want to have it will have it, the rest will be used to make it. Do you all understand?"

"Wait," Soren said, the first word he had spoken since the mission. Fen looked up at him in surprise. "What do you mean by using vampires to make it?"

"The blood," Lorcan replied simply. "That's what the potion needs. I didn't get a full recipe, but it's clear that vampire blood is the main ingredient, and who better to harvest from than lowly Rogues with no house to back them up? It's the perfect crime, truly."

Lorcan was right. It all made sense and it was worse than Soren could have imagined. He didn't know what to do besides kill. His fire would be enough, and he would kill them all if no one else would. Fury rose in his body, searing his nerves.

"Do we know who might be involved?" Trinity asked. "Is there a house that's doing this, or do you think the entire Delegation is responsible?"

Lorcan shook their head. "I don't know. All I know is what these bottles do, and that if something doesn't happen to them soon, every Rogue is finished."

Soren imagined it for a moment, the ability to walk in the sun again. Their bodies turned to dust and blew away in the wind if exposed. If every Royal had it and kept it away from the Rogues, they would have nothing to hold them back. The Royals could open every curtain and let the Rogues all become ash. They could end up like cattle, rotting away forever in a cold room with only dreams to keep them company as their blood became a commodity. It made him sick. Sharing blood between vampires was intimate and sacred, and the Royals forcibly taking it was crossing a vampire line they could not step back behind.

Lorcan dismissed them all, packing up everything and shoving the potions into a backpack, zipping it up and setting it aside. They would bring it to the other Rogues in charge and discuss what to do next. Soren knew what to do. He knew he had to kill the Royals.

-

Fen had not spoken a word on the way to Soren's apartment, only nodding and shaking his head to answer Soren's questions. He wanted to help Fen out of his troubled state, and he wanted to know what caused it. Soren had hoped Fen's blessing was something he'd share with him in due time, but instead it had been forced out of him. Fen had brought him back to life, and Soren was both grateful and guilty. He hoped Fen would not blame himself for his death. Though he could not remember all the details, he knew it had to be his own fault. If only Fen would speak to him, to explain everything, to let him help.

Soren unlocked the door, holding it open for Fen. They were both covered in crusted blood, tear stains still streaking down Fen's cheeks. It would be daylight soon, and they both needed to shower, eat, and sleep. Before anything else, he wanted so badly to just talk. He wanted to touch him, to let him spill words or tears, to do whatever he had to do to make it better. Soren wanted his Fen back. Lovely, sad, and sensitive Fen.

When the door closed and they both kicked off their shoes, Fen stood there, unmoving and blinking down at his feet. Soren stepped closer and embraced him. The tears came immediately, Fen's knees giving way, both of them lowering to the floor as his sobs shook Soren's chest. He held him there, whispering softly and staying steady. Minutes passed. It could have been hours; he did not know. He did not stop holding him. They stayed together on the ground until Fen calmed, his sobs lessening to deep sighs, his body no longer shaking. They remained there; Soren would not let him go until Fen made it so.

Fen clung, his breath evening and his muscles telling a story of fatigue. Soren wondered what the Blessing did to Fen, if it caused him pain or hurt. He hoped it did not. He could not be responsible for any more distress, not to him of all people. There were plenty of others that his rage craved, and Fen did not hold even a whisper of it.

After what felt like a century of silence between them, Fen pulled away just enough to rest his forehead on Soren's shoulder, his words crackling and rasping.

"I'm sorry," he said.

Sorry? What did this miracle have to be sorry for? His angel upon Earth, a being that, if he chose, could say the word and temper Soren's fire to a blade. After what had happened, he almost hoped he would.

"What in the world for?" Soren asked, incredulous.

"Do you remember?" Fen asked back.

He shook his head, afterwards leaning it on the top of Fen's, breathing in his scent. He smelled like smoke and blood and horror.

"Oh," he said, sounding so small.

"I know I died," Soren explained. "And I know you brought me back. That's really all I know."

Fen was silent for a long moment. His fingers gripped the back of Soren's shirt so tightly he thought the fabric might rip.

"It's alright," Soren soothed. "That's all I *need* to know. Details don't matter."

"They do, because the details would tell you that it's my fault!" Fen croaked, his voice so pained that Soren nearly broke.

In truth, he didn't care; he meant what he said. Whatever nonsense Fen was spouting was clearly not the case, and he was being unreasonable to himself.

"It's because of you I'm alive again, so even if it somehow was your fault, I'd say we're even."

"I promised," Fen whispered, more to himself. "I promised and I broke it."

"What promise?"

Fen laughed dryly. "Two, actually. One to myself, and one to Eluvia."

Queen Eluvia? What did she have to do with anything?

"I promised," he said again, his shoulders beginning to tremble again.

It didn't matter. None of it mattered. If it brought Fen pain, he would not allow it.

"Hush," Soren coaxed, rubbing up and down on Fen's back. "We don't have to. I mean it. It's been enough of a ride, and you deserve to take a break."

After a few more moments of comfort, Fen relented. "Okay," he said. "Later."

Soren pulled Fen up with him, and had him sit on the edge of the bed. He slowly began to fish out clothing for Fen to wear from his drawers, setting towels next to him on the bed as well.

"Shower, eat, and rest. Boyfriend's orders," he winked, trying to ease the heaviness.

It worked, if only slightly. Fen picked up the towels, hugging them to his chest as he stood with wide, weary eyes. It felt like he was expecting something.

Soren carried the clothes he picked out to the bathroom, setting them on the counter.

"Feel free to use whatever you want, you go first."

When he turned to leave the bathroom, Fen had not moved. He stood still, waiting.

"What is it?" Soren asked, attempting to keep his worry in check.

Fen bit his lip, his ears turning pink. A swell formed in Soren's heart. That was the Fen he knew.

He waited a moment, going to take a step back to give Fen a bit more space, when a hand shot out and gripped his arm. Fen's hand was cold, hesitant, but did not move.

"Stay," he said, pleading. "Stay with me."

Soren turned to face him. "I'm right here," he said, smiling down at him.

"No," he replied, "I don't want to be alone. Not now."

Understanding donned on him, slowly, carefully.

Sored nodded, retrieving clothes for himself before leading Fen to the shower, the both of them quiet. The air between them still felt thick, like a fog in a forest, but it was thinning every minute.

Fen would feel better, Soren would make sure of it. His hands were fire and brimstone, and he would become calamity. Fen only had to say the word.

Chapter 15

Fen

Fen's head rested on Soren's chest, his damp hair tangled in Soren's fingers. His eyes were open and focused on a point across the room. He did not want to close them. Feeling as content as he could after a meal of hastily made pasta and the blood cartons Soren had provided, he still could not beat back the images in his mind. He felt so weak, so useless in this state. He had never been a fighter—why did he think he would be of any use to the Rogues? His Blessing was not something he used on a whim. It was not something he used at all. When he had seen the trapped vampires and watched Soren die, he knew then he would be only a hindrance. Fen would not go on any more missions that promised danger. Lorcan could use a helper, perhaps. He could assist far better in a room of computers, away from situations that would endanger Soren. He refused to be the reason for his peril, not again.

Soren filled the space with small talk, Fen only responding in nods and shakes of his head. He liked when Soren talked, not about the Rogues or the Sun Potions or Fen's blessing, but of his new favorite Thai food place, the ruined headphones he accidentally ran through the wash, and his desire to get a cat someday. Everything felt so mundane and safe as he spoke, and it drove away some of the thoughts at the forefront of his mind.

He could not ignore them forever, though he wanted nothing more.

Would Soren hate him once he knew? His secrets were meant for him and him alone, but now it was a shared burden. He only hoped the burden would not be too much to bear.

"Soren," he said in a moment of pause.

"Hmm?" Soren purred with a fondness that ached deep in Fen's bones.

"I'm feeling much better right now," Fen said, carefully, testing.

"Good," he replied, squeezing his hold on Fen's waist.

He took a deep breath, still focusing on the wall across the room. "I need to tell you something, and I know it's stupid of me to ask this, but I need to."

Soren's body went a bit stiffer, a seriousness setting in. "Anything," he said, and Fen believed him. It was all the more nerve-wracking.

"Promise you'll try your best not to hate me?"

Soren laughed, breathy and soft. "I promise."

He knew Soren meant it, but that did not change the truth of his life.

"It's about the promises I mentioned. The one to Eluvia. And the one to myself."

And then he began.

-

At twenty-four years old, recently turned, Fen sat on the floor of a dim apartment, back against a wall with peeling paint and the smell of sickness permeating everything around him. An elegant older woman in a deep plum-colored pantsuit knelt down, eye level with him. Her skin was tan, flawless, and shining, with deep brown eyes and sleek hair. Her lips were in a frown, an expression that he was all too familiar with in recent years. Sympathy, pity, condolence. He wished he were dead. He wondered how easy it would be, now that immortality was in his hands. Would his punishment be the inability to escape his actions? It would be fitting, he thought. This beautiful woman did not know him, and he did not know her. He did not care how she had gotten into the apartment shared by him and his Mother.

He did not care how long he had been sitting on the floor, not eating and not drinking. He did not care if he lived.

When her lips parted, the voice that came out was so lilting and lovely it sent shivers down his spine.

"What is your name?" she asked.

"Fen," he said, his voice just barely audible. His throat was so dry he thought it might bleed.

"Lovely," she said, folding her hands together. Her nails were long and glossy, the exact same color as her clothing. "What happened here, love?"

He did not want to answer. He still could not speak of it. Several other people shuffled around the room, but it was as if this woman were all that mattered. The rest of them seemed all but invisible.

She noticed his hesitance.

Waving one of her hands behind her, all the others in the room left. It became so silent he was afraid to breathe.

"It is just us now, my sweet. Come, it will be good to tell someone."

He did not want to. He did not know her, but he wanted to.

"Who are you?" he asked.

She smiled again, this time more warmly. "You will not know what this entails, but I am called Queen Eluvia. You, child, may call me Eluvia. Speak when you wish, and I can promise a life far better than the one you left as a mortal."

"I don't want to," he said, pained, desperate. "I don't want a life. Kill me."

Her hand came to rest on his shoulder, firm and attentive. "I will not. Tell me what happened here in this sad place. You will feel better. I promise."

He believed her.

-

At twenty-three years old, still mortal, Fen sat in a hospital waiting room, nearly picking his fingers bloody as he watched the TV in the corner of the room. When a doctor in a pristine white coat walked to him, he did not make eye contact. The doctor spoke words to him he did not want to hear, and he did not respond. He knew he should, but he could not bring himself to. Not until the doctor asked, "Do you want to see her?"

He did.

They walked to a sterile room, his Mother in a bed of white sheets that looked too stiff for her. He could bring blankets from home—the ones she'd brought from China before coming to America and having him. The ones she clung to when his Father left, his humorless green eyes all Fen could remember now. The blankets would smell like home, not like chemicals and sickness.

He sat at her bedside, her sunken face as warm as she could muster. Fen had asked for a moment to speak with her alone. It was just the two of them, the windows open to a gray and dismal rain outside. He wondered how many more rainy days she had left before banishing the thought.

"Oh, my boy," she said, her grip on his hand weaker than he had ever felt. "Did the doctor tell you? He is a nice man, so kind."

Fen nodded.

"I will stay here, that is better. The doctor said so and I agree. You go back to school, my boy, they have internet here for calls."

He would not. He had already dropped out. He would not tell her.

"Mama," he said softly. "What do you want me to bring from home? I can bring your blankets, I can bring them tomorrow."

149

Her smile turned sad, so sad and so tired. "What will you do after tomorrow?" she asked.

He would stay. He would not leave his Mother alone, dying, slowly becoming a husk of skin. He did not care if she did not want him to. He would stay.

"I have a job, Mama. I'll come when I'm not working, we can watch that show you started."

He lied. He did not have a job. He would not even have a Mother soon enough.

"Good," she said. "What about school?"

He shook his head. "Taking a break for now. I'll stay here until you get healthy enough to come home."

Her eyes said everything he needed to know, everything he already knew. She did not argue. When he left the hospital, he vomited outside in the bushes. His hands shook on the steering wheel of his Mother's car. Fen would go home, lie in bed on his laptop, and search for something. He did not care what. He would find a way to keep her alive. He would do anything.

-

At twenty-four years old, in his last moments of mortality, Fen sat in a peeling leather chair in a stranger's home.

She was biting his neck, and he was half hoping it would kill him. He had followed connection after connection, finding this woman across the city who claimed she was a vampire. She claimed she could turn others into vampires. She said vampires held incredible powers that could do anything. Fen would do anything.

His eyes were fixed on the ceiling, a horribly cold sensation stemming from fangs on his throat. It was frigid, the icy feeling so white-hot it burned. His veins felt like they were filled to the brim, about to pop within his body. Maybe they did. All at once, he felt like he was floating, and then dropped suddenly. The air pushed out of his lungs, ears ringing and eyes blinking away tears. The pain was absolute, then over in an instant. The woman pulled away, wiping her mouth, then holding out her hand.

"Pay up," she ordered.

He did.

He left, shaking in the driver's seat of his Mother's car. He shook all the way to the hospital. He shook as he walked past the staff, carrying his mother in his arms as she sleepily asked what he was doing, where they were going. He shook as he pushed past everybody who stood in his way.

His Mother was light as a feather; carrying her up the two flights of stairs to their apartment was no different than carrying a plastic bag. That's all she felt like: hollow, crinkling plastic. She questioned less and less the higher they went, her energy slipping away with each step. In the time she stayed at the hospital, she had only gotten worse. She was gray, limbs thin and stringy, no muscle left to aid her in walking or doing much of anything. Her voice sounded like wind being forced through a tube. Her hair was all but gone, just some wispy strings clinging to her head here and there. The color of her whole body was nothing. She was nothing.

He had the power to fix her now.

Fen set her on her bed, kept clean and tidy as he awaited this day.

He realized his mother was crying.

It did not matter. It would all be better soon enough.

He had practiced on the stray cats that he found dead around the city, even a large dog, once. Fen did not know how he figured out his power. It was as if once he became a vampire, the knowledge came with it. He had still practiced, always freshly dead bodies, making sure once it came time for his mother, he would be confident. It had to be perfect. He would fix her.

Time passed and he did not keep track. It did not feel like long. His mother could not bring herself back to the hospital, and did not seem to care enough anymore, now that she was home. She had given up, relishing in the last of her life spent in the home they shared. He cared for her day and night, feeding her, cleaning her, watching shows and reading magazines with her. She seemed happy.

Her death came with the morning sun. The curtains were closed, casting her body in foggy shade. Fen stood over her, checking her heart, her pulse, everything to make sure she was truly gone. He did not weep. He did not need to. He would fix her.

His hands rested on her chest, above her heart, and light pulsed from him like it had all the times before. He urged, pleaded, pushed, and pulled as hard as he could.

"Follow."

And she woke up.

And she was still sick.

And she looked at him like she did not know him.

She knew she had died. Her peace with it had come months ago, her death coming closer and her regrets fading. She had told him so, but he had not cared. He fixed her.

But she was no longer warm towards him. She still had to be fed and cleaned, and while she still breathed, she was miserable.

Her death came again.

Fen brought her back again.

She looked at him like he was a demon.

"My boy," she sobbed. "What happened to you?"

Her sobs wracked her whole body, there was no weight to hold her steady.

Fen wanted to scream. "I fixed you!" he retorted, his eyes dewy.

She shook her head, and it seemed to take all her strength.

"My boy would let me rest," she said, and her voice held more pity than he had ever heard. "He would live."

The tears came, hot and abundant. They fell to the floor at his feet where he stood, fists clenched at his sides. "Not without you!" he cried.

"I will die again," she stated, as casually as the times she had called him for dinner as a child. "You know this. Let me go, my boy."

"I can't," he said. "I won't."

"You must."

Her third death came on a rainy day.

He stood over her, putting his hands on her chest. The light came. He said the word.

She opened her eyes, and they were cold.

They were so cold he staggered back from her, his back to the wall.

She looked at him for so long that he thought he had calcified. He waited until she spoke, her voice so weak and so full of disdain.

"You are not my boy," she said. "I do not know who you are. My boy would let me rest."

She went to sleep, and Fen stayed pinned to the wall, sinking down with his head in his knees. He screamed. He cried. He did not sleep and did not eat. He moved from the bedroom only when her death came for the fourth and last time, shortly after she had sunk into her nap. He covered her with her blankets before settling in the living room. He sat on the floor, facing the front door, against the wall.

He stayed like that until Eluvia came.

"Tell me what happened here in this sad place," she said. "You will feel better. I promise."

He did not know how he could ever feel better, but he believed her all the same. Fen told her all that had happened, feeling as though his very being was made only of tears and shaking and regret. Eluvia's hand on his shoulder had squeezed, comforting, and he imagined it was his Mother instead.

"I am so sorry, child," she said. "Come with me now, you will have a place to heal."

As he stood up, Eluvia's strength doing all the work as her hands gripped his arms, he said only one thing before following the Queen wherever she was taking him.

"I couldn't fix her."

-

After days of meals and showers and blood, Fen had a room made up for him in Eluvia's castle. It was everything he had ever dreamed. He wondered what would happen when he opened the curtains during the day, ending his wretched life for good. He planned on it that day.

Fen was escorted to Eluvia's study and left there alone with her. Since being adopted into her Royal House, he had been given a rundown of basic protocol. A vampire named Lorcan had been telling him everything, seemingly becoming his caretaker. He hoped Lorcan would not be too hurt once Fen died. Writing them a note would have to be enough.

Eluvia gestured for him to sit in the seat across from her at the desk. He did so, placing his hands in his lap and looking down at them.

"Fen," she said sweetly, so sweetly it made his chest tighten. "How are you liking it here? Is your new room all you hoped it would be?"

He nodded simply.

"I am glad," she said, leaning her chin on folded hands, elbows propping her arms up. "I am here for any wish and desire you request. You need only say the word, and all will be yours."

Fen wanted nothing but death. It was all he needed.

"I know what you truly want I cannot give," she began, tone beautiful and solemn. "And I am sorry for that. Just know that if I could, my sweet, I would."

"Why?" asked Fen, more bitter than he meant for it to sound.

She paused, eyes so focused on Fen it made him squirm. "Why what, darling?"

"Why am I here?" he asked. "Why take me in?"

He heard a shuffling as Eluvia got up, dragged her chair over next to his, and sat down elegantly on it. One of her hands rested on his, her nails now navy to match her slim, formal dress. He wondered what she was so finely dressed for.

"Fen, lovely child, the answer is so simple I am afraid you may not believe it," she said almost sheepishly. "I took you in because you needed it. You needed someone, and I saw in you everything you do not seem to see in yourself. Believe me or do not, but I do not care so deeply for most of the vampires in my care. I have many here for more... political reasons."

Her hand squeezed his, and he was shocked to find himself so rapt.

"You are not here for that reason, Fen. You are here because I wish for you to be. I cannot promise your Mother, but I can promise to be here for you however you require. You need only stay, and live however you wish."

Fen did not know how or why, but her offer was starting to sound good. He knew this woman for only a short time, yet he believed her every word. She was kind, and she was there for him. Perhaps that was what he needed. Dying may not be his only path. Death was becoming a hazier and hazier thought, but it felt wrong to let himself live. Why did he deserve such a lavish life of happiness and contentment?

"Why?" he asked again.

Queen Eluvia turned his chair to face her, fingers feather-light on his chin, turning his gaze to her eyes.

"You are far finer a young man than you realize. I simply see that, and hope you shall come to see it, too, in due time."

Fen wanted to feel better, and he wanted to move on. He wanted to believe her, so he let himself.

"Okay," he said, gulping away the emotion that threatened to loose from his throat. "I'll stay."

She nodded happily, though she did not release his chin.

"That is wonderful! As I said, you need only speak what you desire, and I shall have it done."

Her pause then became charged. Fen felt like everything around them was frozen in ice, all energy on hold. Her deep brown eyes bore into his, not unkindly, though they lacked the warmth from before.

Eluvia's next words came to his ears like every syllable was laced in sweets and fulfillment. They felt like a cake in the middle of the night, the first drink on a night out, honey on bread. Fen listened like it was the only sound he had ever heard.

"There is only one thing I require of you," she said, all sugar and loveliness. "I do not think it will ever come to pass, but I ask for it nonetheless. In the event of my death, one that allows for it, I consent to life. Will you do this for me?"

He did not want to do it ever again. The images and words of his Mother flashed like a hot iron pressed against his skull. It became a horrid flood, and it nearly caused him to double over in pain. His Blessing was a curse; he would never use it again. He could not. He had promised himself after his Mother's final death.

Eluvia's voice silenced it all. Fen did not know how, but he was grateful, more grateful for the silence than anything else that had been done for him thus far. He gasped in air, eyes focused back on the Queen as she spoke.

"I can banish those thoughts as many times as you need. I only ask for your promise, nothing more."

And he did. He promised her. She would be the only one he would ever bring back again, and life became a series of days and years, memories fading to a dull throb of pain rather than a bleeding wound.

Until Soren.

Chapter 16

Soren

The cold bathroom counter under Soren's fingers did not feel solid enough to keep him steady. Water in the sink ran and ran, the sound ringing out into biting silence. It did nothing to calm his mind, yet he watched. He splashed his face with it for the third time, droplets hanging at his chin before falling, creating pools that spilled over into the bowl. Fen was in the bed outside, sleeping soundly in the dark. Soren checked his phone; it was late afternoon. The sun would still be too high for any vampire to wake, but the Rogue could not sleep.

His thoughts mimicked the water his eyes hazily focused on, the liquid at full speed pushing from the spout, and leaving through the drain just as fast. He could not grasp any solid thought before it slipped through his fingers.

After Fen told him about his Mother and his promise to Eluvia, Soren had become many things. He was sad, angry, horrified, but most of all, he no longer knew what he wanted for his own life. Fen was the only constant, the only sure thing he could imagine. The rest all blended together like a mirage—hazy,

161

dissipating. His hatred, his need for revenge on the Royals, his urge to tear it all down—it all no longer felt as important as it once had. Were his last twenty-three years as a vampire wasted? All thrown away on schemes and missions and fires? What would have happened if he had met Fen sooner?

Soren turned the sink off, the sudden quiet swallowing the space in its absence. It wasn't that he felt the Royals should be left alone, or that the current events were to be ignored. But, for the first time since being turned, he asked himself, *Why me*? Why had he assigned himself the role of the hero? Why had he thought he was the only one who could take them all down? It had been the only thing keeping his second life going, the only goal, the only reason he lived. Hatred was a hell of a motivator.

Was that still his purpose? Did he still want it to be his reason for breathing? He could not abandon the Rogues, not now. But what about after?

What if he had a new reason to live?

The thought shocked him to his core, and he nearly doubled back into the wall. He was becoming someone else, and he wasn't sure yet if he liked this new Soren. The vampire staring back at him from the mirror felt unfamiliar, with the green strand of hair dyed to match Fen's eyes that hadn't turned out right. Although he'd tried to capture their beauty, it couldn't compare.

The soft red marks on his neck and chest were fading, remnants of tender moments he would starve for. He heard rustling in the bed, and then silence once more.

The Prince in his bed meant something to him, but he wasn't sure if he meant more than Soren's revenge. His hatred of Royals ran deep, and for the first time, he felt a spark of hope—hope that Fen may be enough to rewrite what felt etched into his very core.

Soren tore his eyes away from the mirror, flipped the light switch off, and gently opened the door. He peeked out from the doorway, narrowing his eyes to focus on the lump of blankets a few feet away. The Rogue decided he would not think too hard about it, for the time being. Instead, he would focus on crawling back into bed, settling himself behind Fen, and wrapping his arms around him. There had been more tears, soft whispers of comfort, and a seething disquiet kept hidden in Soren's chest. Fen thought of Eluvia as a second mother, his savior, the one person responsible for healing him. Soren knew better. He had no proof, but he would in time. Queen Eluvia was cunning first and foremost, and Soren would tear her apart for it. He wanted nothing more than to see his flames swallow her, for her reign over Fen to end in smoke. Soren would kill her, he had to. For Fen.

He only hoped Fen would see the truth when it came. He could not bear what would come if Fen did not forgive him.

-
.

The alarm on Soren's phone rang only once before Fen's pale hand shot out from under the covers to turn it off, before promptly settling back to his previous position. Soren could not help himself, and a small chuckle vibrated in his chest against Fen's back.

Fen grumbled, but said nothing.

"Good waking to you, too," Soren whispered, nuzzling his face into the back of Fen's neck.

He shivered. "Let me sleep," he begged, voice raspy.

"Hand me my phone, then," said Soren. "I need to check for any news."

Fen wordlessly grabbed the cell phone and plopped it into Soren's open hand.

"Thank you, darling," Soren teased.

Fen gave a grunt of approval.

Opening his notifications was like a cut to his stomach, and anxiety oozed out of the wound. Lorcan had sent a text stating simply that there was to be a meeting, and that further details would be discussed. It was in three hours. He only had three more hours of grumpy waking Fen, of the sliver of normalcy he so desperately wanted more of. Reaching over Fen, Soren put his phone face down on the bedside table. The Prince caught his arm before he could retract it, wrapping it around his bare chest and lacing his fingers with Soren's.

"No more alarms," Fen said into his pillow.

"No more alarms," Soren agreed.

Three more hours.

He knew he needed to tell Fen. Would it be so wrong to wait? Just so he could keep the peace as long as he could?

Without realizing, Soren had begun to shuffle his feet, disturbing Fen enough for him to sigh and turn his body to face him.

"What are you thinking about?" he asked, and his face was so soft. He was so beautiful.

Soren had to look away; it was too much beauty for him, and it would blind him one of these days.

"Soren," Fen urged, touching their foreheads together. "I talked my soul out of my body yesterday, the least you can do is tell me what's on your mind."

He was right, and he was so lovely.

"I got a text from Lorcan," Soren said finally, closing his eyes. "There's a meeting in three hours."

"Ah," Fen said dryly. "I thought maybe we'd have a little more time."

He was radiant, even in the dark, even with messy hair and sleepy eyes.

"I did, too," Soren whispered.

Fen rested both hands on the back of Soren's neck, rubbing his thumbs along his skin. "I'll have to go home at some point before you leave."

"Yeah," Soren said, so sadly that he surprised even himself.

Three more hours. He was so pretty, like a forest in the rain, melancholic and deep.

"But that's in three hours," Fen said, his tone brightening just enough. "We still have time."

Soren nodded, his arms wrapping in an embrace as he pulled Fen close, breathing in his scent, touching his skin. Would this stunning man be the end of him? When death came to claim him a final time, he could think of no sweeter way to meet it.

-

166

"I'll program the directions again," Lorcan explained to the room of Rogues.

There were more than Soren had ever seen in one mission meeting, at least fifteen gathered together and packed like matches, so tense they may all alight any moment.

Lorcan had scanned the stolen documents top to bottom, side to side, and done who-knows-what to gather leads. Soren never knew what exactly they did, but it had always worked. He never asked, and never needed to. Soren was the bullet, and Lorcan the one firing.

They were speaking fast, dominantly, and without making eye contact with a single one of them. Soren knew why. He yearned for Lorcan to look at him, to feel the lava in his gaze. But they knew better.

The leads had pointed to Queen Eluvia's castle. *Big shocker*, Soren thought. It was all the proof he needed for his conviction. The only thing on his mind was whether Fen would see it the same way. It frightened him to no end that he was not sure.

As the Rogues all began to shuffle about, grabbing gear and weapons, Soren strode directly to Lorcan the moment a path opened. He had questions, and he would get answers.

Lorcan saw him coming, and their gaze turned icy.

"Lorcan," Soren whispered through his teeth. "Does he know?"

They huffed, crossing their legs and leaning back in their chair. "Of course not."

"Why the fuck not?" he hissed.

"Because he won't even be in the castle. He doesn't need to know anything anymore, not after what you made him do." They paused, making sure their words were concise. "He will be safe, and he will be away from your chaos."

Soren's hands became hot, feverishly so. He could not help his actions, not when Lorcan was so clearly provoking him. He would not take it.

One of his hands shot out, grabbing the collar of Lorcan's shirt. At least, that's what should've happened. Instead, his hand phased through them, akin to a hologram. His eyes widened, darting around the room to see if any of the Rogues had noticed. Most were already out and heading to their cars, the rest too preoccupied to notice.

Lorcan sighed deeply, rubbing two fingers along their temple. "I'm taking care of it, you just keep your hands to yourself and do the mission. It's simple, you should be able to handle that."

"No!" Soren spat, crossing his arms. "You answer me. What the hell was that just now, and what are you doing with Fen?"

"My Blessing," they began, tone casual, like Soren wasn't brimming with rage above them, "is the answer to both of those questions."

"Elaborate."

"Why?"

"Fuck, Lorcan, why is it like pulling teeth with you right now? Just answer me and I'll leave."

They thought for a moment, tapping a foot on the floor. It was infuriating.

"Fine," they decided. "My Blessing is making a double of myself. The real me is out with Fen right now, and this is the double sitting before you. Are you able to comprehend it all now? Or shall I repeat myself?"

It was a hell of a Blessing, Soren had to admit. He wondered how many times Lorcan had truly been in person at meetings, or if it had all been their double.

"How are you sitting in that chair then?" he asked.

Lorcan rolled their eyes, trying to go for annoyance, but it felt flat. They seemed more tired than anything. "I can interact with objects, but not sentient beings. Are you done?"

"Where are you bringing Fen?"

"Not telling."

"Lorcan," Soren said, and he let his voice turn from cold to pleading. For Fen, he would throw his pride away and never pick it back up. "Please."

Lorcan opened their mouth to speak, and then their eyes seemed to fog over, their head turning up towards the ceiling. Just as quickly, their head lowered, eyes clear and full of panic.

A million thoughts raced in Lorcan's mind. Soren could see it on their face. His skin prickled as he watched them, a feeling of unease growing like a rash, making his skin hot and itchy.

Lorcan looked at Soren with a seriousness that made him forget to breathe. It was paralyzing.

"I have to go," they said, their voice rushed. "Get to the castle. Eluvia is back early."

Chapter 17

Fen

Fen flung his body onto his bed, closed his eyes, and just breathed for a few minutes. He felt like a weight had been lifted, and another materialized to take its place. It had felt right to tell Soren about his past, but he could tell the Rogue had something deep in his mind that Fen could not see the bottom of. He still knew nothing of Soren's life before, why he hated the Royals so much, or why he had seemed so forlorn when they had woken. Soren had given him space to tell him on his own terms. Fen wanted to do the same for Soren, but he felt as though a timer was set, and once it counted down, a piece of Soren may be lost. It was painful, seeing the anger under Soren's skin anytime trigger words were said. He feared it would burn Soren from the inside.

Before his mind fully immersed itself in thought, Fen heard a knock at his door. He had hoped his solitude would stretch longer, but a second knock had him sighing and rising from his bed. He opened the heavy wooden door just a crack, a flash of auburn hair catching his eye first. The door opened wider as he saw Lorcan, a smile upon their freckled face.

"Lorcan?" he asked, puzzled. "What're you doing here?"

"Coming to take you out!" they said, grinning. "You desperately need some time outside. Live a little! I'm just here to oblige."

"Why aren't you at the meeting?" Fen whispered, making sure no one else was walking the hallway.

Lorcan laughed, shaking their head. "I'm not leading that one. I have a friend who needs to have a good time; I think that warrants my attention far more."

Someone else was leading the meeting? Fen supposed it could be true, but it felt wrong. The whole interaction felt wrong. It made him squeeze his hands into defiant fists and he tried for a serious tone.

"Don't lie."

Lorcan's eyes faltered for a split second, and it was enough.

Fen went to shut his door, his patience spent, but Lorcan held it open.

"Fen," they said, "I'm sorry. I just don't think that's the best topic for you at the moment."

"Whatever."

"Fen!" Lorcan was flustered, but gripped the door tightly. "Seriously, I mean it. I do want to take you out to get your mind off of things. The double is at the meeting, okay? That's the truth, I swear."

The double, of course. Fen touched Lorcan's shoulder just to test, and it was the real thing. It was a start.

"Just come out," they pleaded, pouting their lower lip. "Please?"

Fen had to admit, the idea of taking a walk sounded nice, the cool night breeze and warm street lamps beckoning. He could forget the sadness in Soren's eyes, if just for a little while, and get an iced coffee to drown the taste of worry on his tongue. Fen wanted to feel normal again, as much as could be achieved.

"Let me change," he replied, watching Lorcan's face light up.

"Great!" they said. "I'll wait, but not too long, or else I'll leave without you."

They wouldn't. Fen knew it, and he smiled.

He closed the door and went to his wardrobe, picking out ripped black jeans and a knit sweater striped with orange and black. He slid his leather boots on, checking himself in the mirror. His hair was more of a disaster than he thought, and he cursed Soren silently for messing it up. After redoing the half-up

173

hairstyle he frequented, he opened the door to Lorcan leaning against the wall, face lit by their phone screen. It was their expression that stopped him in his doorway. Fear.

Lorcan looked to Fen, a decision balancing on their lips. Fen held his breath.

"It's too late," they whispered. "She's back."

-

Fen didn't understand anything that was happening. Eluvia had come back early, and for some reason, Lorcan was pale and silent about it. They both sat in her office, her hair severe in a flowing ponytail on her head, dark eyes glittering like jewels. Her face was the picture of neutrality, neither happy nor upset. Fen could not wrap his mind around the air in the room, the tenseness suffocating as Lorcan sat, stiff and serious. It felt like the eye of a storm on the precipice of rupturing, if only he reached out to touch it. He decided he would.

"Eluvia," he began, trying to be casual. "Why the summons?"

The Queen's gaze did not move from Lorcan, a fierce focus that felt much like a bird of prey, steadfast in her eyes.

Lorcan did not speak. Eluvia did not speak. Fen shuffled in his seat as the silence became unbearable.

"Lorcan?" Fen tried, turning a kind gaze to his friend. "Earth to Lorcan?"

"My dear Fen," cooed Eluvia, voice thick and soft like cashmere, warm on a winter's evening. "Do you have anything to tell me?"

He blinked, dazed. It felt like his mind was being cocooned, hugged in softness and honey. The feeling was both disorienting and lovely.

Lorcan spoke before Fen got the chance. "My Queen–"

"I did not ask you, my sweet." Interrupted Eluvia. "Your time will come."

Fen's thoughts became hazier with each passing second, a fog surrounding him that made all his nerves loosen. He did not want to speak anymore—he felt wrong, and he felt blissful.

Lorcan's voice sounded again, doing little to uncloud Fen's confusion. "Please, my Queen, I beg you. I have the answers you seek. Fen is just a lovesick puppy, he has nothing useful to tell."

What was Lorcan saying? It felt insulting, but Fen could not conjure any negative emotions. They were locked away deep within him, somewhere he could not reach.

"Lovesick?" Eluvia mused, speaking like Fen was not in front of her. "That may be so. I know you have what I seek, but you have a much higher wall to scale."

She paused, considering.

"No matter," she said finally, her eyes turning to Fen, and all his fogginess evaporated in an instant. He gasped, overwhelmed by the return of all his emotions, his fingers gripping the arms of his chair.

Lorcan sighed in relief, resolve written on their freckled face.

"My sweet," Eluvia whispered, and Lorcan's body eased. "You have been working diligently. I see all here, and so you leave the castle for your work. It blinds me, for a time. But I still have ears, my child. I hear your whispers and your schemes and they are so very quiet. I left you to your own devices for far too long. Your fun is over."

Fen could not follow her speech, the hair on the back of his neck bristling, his confusion and nerves prickling on his skin. He looked to Lorcan, and while their body was loose, their eyes were hard as stone.

"Lorcan," Eluvia spoke again, her voice more commanding. "How much does Fen know?"

Their eyes flicked to Fen, then forward again as they swallowed. "Not all."

Eluvia nodded. "That is still too much, I'm afraid. You have brought it upon yourself, my sweet Lorcan. Do not forget this."

Fen was confused, so confused, and so afraid. Eluvia had never elicited such fear from him, and it made his stomach twist and turn. She was kind, she was his second mother, and she was terrifying.

Her deep brown eyes bore into his, sympathy permeating the air. "I am sorry, truly. You were not meant for this, and yet Lorcan dragged you into the depths of their own mistakes. I regret that you must lose the one you have come to hold dear, but you have eternity to rewrite your heart."

Fen's blood ran cold.

"Lorcan," she said, their name feeling electrified, coursing through the room. "Take Fen away. He needs time to himself, time to heal."

Lorcan said nothing. They stood, gripped Fen's arm, and yanked him to his feet. Their grip was hard, their fingers quivering.

Fen startled at the contact, the grasp of his friend so tight it felt bruising. His mind reeled so fast he thought it may cease to work entirely. He did not know what to say, so he said anything that would come to his tongue.

"What do you mean?" he cried, voice rising with every word. "Eluvia, Lorcan, I don't know what's going on and I'm scared. Please tell me, tell me anything. Please don't be mad at me."

His voice was breaking, his heart was breaking, and his mind was breaking.

"Eluvia, please, where am I going? What is happening? I'm scared, I'm scared," and he repeated those words. As Lorcan dragged him to the door, his willpower too weak to fight back, his knees buckled and he kneeled on the ground. His head fell into his hands, tears hot on his fingers. The flashes of all the recent events of his life were like a hot iron, burning and burning. Everything stung so deeply.

Elegant heels came into his blurred view of the floor, and a hand rested atop his head. The touch was soft, so soft.

He looked up, and Eluvia was before him, almost eye level.

Fen's crying stopped the moment he saw her face. Any affection she had ever held in her gaze towards him was gone. It was so powerful he imagined for a moment that she had never loved him at all. He knew it was not true. It couldn't be.

Her eyes did not change. Her voice commanded, and he could not disobey.

"Sleep," she said simply, and so he did. The last image burned into his memories was of Eluvia's lips parting to speak, her expression one of utter annoyance, and he thought he might as well die then and there.

Chapter 18

Soren

They burned and they burned, bodies melting into the walls and floors, the smell of acrid vampire flesh becoming ash all that Soren breathed. His hands would not calm, flames kissing any skin that deigned to come close. Soren thought as his palm slammed into the face of another Royal vampire, eyes bursting like so many fireworks, that this is what love feels like. He understood the violence of it: all the years of fires, and he knew now what the feeling was. Love kissed his mind and body and burned him just the same. Images of moss and forests seared his insides like the heat from his fingertips that exploded into the hair of a vampire he did not see the face of, the strands quickly alighting like a fuse. She screamed, and he only heard it in the back of his consciousness. The forefront of his senses held only soft blushes and black nails on delicate fingers, a red dragon tattoo under his grasp, and rasping breaths upon his neck. Death was so like life, and Soren had never cared which end of the string he was tied to. Love had made him tie the string around his neck, and he would keep it from strangling him as long as Fen still breathed. He would do anything.

Trinity was behind him, shouting for him, telling him to slow down. She was fighting her own battles, dodging panicked, flame-covered bodies patting themselves down with blistered hands, desperate to calm the heat. Soren would not let them. The Royals had no judge, no court of law to keep them from causing pain. Soren would be the executioner; it was all he could do. He did not care that tapestries were dropping embers onto the rugs, the walls and floors slowly becoming the hall to Hell. Trinity would just have to keep up. They would all have to keep up. Soren would not be kept.

The door to Eluvia's study was in sight. Soren's gaze focused on nothing else. The Royals kept coming, running in one of two directions: towards Soren, where only death would greet them, and away down the hall, where they could live another night. He wished he could kill them all, but Fen was waiting for him, and giving chase to the stragglers was unimportant. Trinity's hand on his shoulder, trying to yank him to face her, was unimportant. Every word she said was unimportant.

Soren let his hands cool as he gripped the handle of the study, knuckles white. He breathed in deeply, smoke and burning bodies filling his lungs. His eyes were wild, his senses turned up as far as they could go. What waited behind the door was enough to send him into a frenzy, one he would gladly unleash.

He turned the handle and flung open the door.

"Oh dear," a velvety voice said. "Quite the mess you've made."

Sitting with linked hands, chin resting upon them, and a smile on perfect dark lips, was Eluvia. She was the only other vampire in the room, and she seemed to fill every inch with her presence. The Queen was lovely, with tan skin and deep eyes that looked only at Soren as he stood, frozen one step into the room. He felt his legs tremble, and he gritted his teeth. What was he so afraid of? He needed to kill her. This would be his best chance, and he needed to take it. Fen would have to forgive him later. He had to.

"Sit," Eluvia ordered, and the word was like a gong in Soren's ears, the feeling of it echoing in every crevice of his skull.

His legs trembled again as he tried to move, trying to lunge at the Royal in front of him, but his body would not listen to his commands.

"And shut the door behind you, that smoke is quite unpleasant."

The door clicked shut behind him as his hand moved without his leave. He heard Trinity outside, feet getting closer to the door. She would arrive in moments, and it would snap Soren out of whatever was happening to him. He tried to wait, but Eluvia would not have it.

"Troublesome one, sit."

His fingers shook, and his feet slid across the floor, dragging him to the chair opposite the Queen. Soren's entire body screamed and shook as fire built in his hands. He would place his fire upon her as soon as he was close enough. She would burn like the rest.

Eluvia tsked as Soren sat, his shaking hand about to reach for her. "Hold your fire, young one. You have done quite enough."

Soren's hands began to dim, and his eyes unfocused as he used all his willpower to urge the flames back up. They would not. His body was not his own.

"Good," the Queen cooed, leaning back in her chair and folding her hands in her lap. "This will not take long. I do not have the time to keep you at bay indefinitely. I will give you credit where it is due; you are challenging."

Soren wanted to spit fire onto her. He wanted to watch as her life blackened into nothing.

"This much of my Blessing has not been used in a long while," Eluvia continued. "You are every bit as wondrous as I was told. A true force of nature, you are. It is a shame your hatred binds you so tightly. If only you had accepted the offer before you years ago, perhaps your life with Fen here could have come true. I would have gained power in my House that few would want to tangle with."

Eluvia's eyes would not leave Soren's, her gaze stone-still and just as strong. He felt nauseous.

"Alas, you dealt your own cards. There is no one to blame but yourself."

The door to the study shook, the handle turning rapidly, and it flung open.

Trinity was there, panting as she looked from Eluvia to Soren and back again.

"They're gone," Trinity said to Soren, her hands reaching for him. "They're on the way to the facility, we need to go—"

Eluvia's eyes became cold. They were so cold that Soren felt his spine harden and his blood freeze. Fear.

"Kill her," Eluvia said simply.

Soren's hand burst to life, swinging it behind him, gripping Trinity's shirt.

He could not look. He could not see. His eyes blurred. Was he crying? Soren could not tell, he could not think. Trinity was burning and she was burning and she was screaming.

Between Trinity's cries, Eluvia looked back to Soren, and raised her voice so Soren could hear her.

"You tire me, boy. Sleep."

He fought a battle inside of himself, his whole body wracked with shaking he could not keep at bay. His eyes began to drift shut, the heat in his hands smoldering to nothing.

Before his consciousness left him, Soren looked at Eluvia's face. Her skin was wet with sweat, and her breathing was ragged. It looked as if all her energy was being used to keep herself upright. Her shaking hand lifted a phone to her ear.

"Bring me blood," she said, voice strained. "This one was a challenge. I will need rest. Tell the Delegation I have him."

Soren smiled madly as blackness enveloped his vision. The image of the invincible Queen was cracked. At least he had been a challenge for her.

Chapter 19

Fen

No dreams came to Fen in his forced sleep. No thoughts raced in his mind, no fear, and no confusion. It would be his last moment of peace before his consciousness caught up.

He awoke slowly, bleary blinks clouding his vision. A soft, warm light cast shadows upon stark white walls, stiff blankets covered his body, and the eerie silence surrounding him let him know he was in a place he did not know. As his eyes focused, he sat up, rubbing his face and taking shallow, shaky breaths. He did not want to look. He did not want to know. He did not want to be alive at that moment.

Ignoring the pit in his stomach, Fen lifted his face to gaze around the room. He nearly vomited.

An observation window sat across the room with curtains drawn, though he could see shadows pass behind the fabric. He was in a small metal bed with hospital sheets, and one lone desk lamp sat on the floor as his only source of light. Nothing else was with him there. His phone was not in any of his pockets, though he checked feverishly for it. There was a metal door just steps away, and he knew it would not open. He knew he was trapped. He tried regardless.

His hands twisted the handle, pounded on the door, and eventually slunk down to his sides. Fen's feet carried him back to the bed where he curled into himself atop the hard mattress, trying not to cry. No tears came. All he could do was lie with closed eyes, hoping that sleep would claim him once more, and that he would dream. Would he dream of Eluvia, of the last look he had seen on her face? Maybe he would dream of Soren, laughing and languid with his fingers in Fen's hair. If his mind turned against him just enough, he would dream of his Mother.

A minute or a day could have passed—Fen did not care to count—until the door handle slowly turned. Lifting his head, he held his breath, digging nails into his palms. *Please be Soren*, he wished.

A disheveled Lorcan stood in the doorway, holding a carton of blood and wearing a look Fen could not place. As they shut the door behind them, Fen tried to make himself smaller, small enough to disappear. Lorcan was not phased as they hesitantly sat on the bed next to Fen, holding out the carton.

"Here," they said, voice hoarse but caring.

Fen did not move.

Lorcan sighed and set the blood onto the bed in front of Fen.

A silence stretched between them, one that Fen was glad of. He did not want to open his mouth for fear of what may come out.

Lorcan did not have the same concerns. "I'm sorry about before," they said. "And I'm sorry about right now, too. I tried to convince Eluvia to let you stay somewhere more... homey, but I'm not her favorite right now."

Fen did not speak.

That seemed to bother Lorcan, as their tone became more terse. "I'm lucky to be alive right now, and you're lucky you have a bed here. No one else does, just so you know."

Fen was beginning to feel rage bubbling within him, white-hot and ugly. He felt like he understood nothing, and Lorcan would still not give him any answers. Why should he care about their feelings?

"Look," Lorcan began, sighing and trying to slip back into a more casual voice. "I know this place is awful, but the castle isn't exactly in the best shape right now, so the facility is the best option. Especially to keep you safe right now. You just need time; time to cool off and time to come to your senses. You'll be let out soon, I'm sure, so just sit tight for now."

Fuck his safety, and fuck whatever Lorcan was hiding. Fen would not keep quiet any longer. He would tear the place apart.

"Let me out," he seethed.

Lorcan startled, not expecting to hear anything in the pause between them. "I can't, not yet," they said. "Things are shit right now, flaming castles and Delegation calls are all anyone can focus on. You need to stay here until it blows over. You shouldn't have been involved in any of this to begin with, but your pyromaniac boyfriend made sure you got knee-deep in it all. I'm just trying to make sure it doesn't cover your head."

The mention of Soren had Fen reeling, seething. His body shook.

Lorcan rested a hand on his shoulder. "This is for the best. You have infinite time to be happy again, I will make sure of it, Eluvia too. Soren could have been good for you in another life, but in this one, he only brings you danger. I know you see it."

His flame, his ruby, his forest fire. Soren, Soren, Soren.

"I'm sorry it hurts right now, but it won't hurt forever. I'm here for you, and soon you'll be out and about, in daylight even! Imagine!"

189

Daylight at the cost of Rogue blood, at the cost of the vampires who had no choice.

"I was helping the Rogues because I knew Eluvia was up to something," Lorcan explained. "I was worried it would destroy the balance of everything. The Sun Potions come from... less than ideal circumstances, but Fen, they could make you happy. They could change our world, make us borderline invincible. You could be on a date with some hot guy in the *daytime*, wouldn't that be amazing?"

"Why?" Fen asked, shifting his body so Lorcan's hand was no longer touching him.

Lorcan blinked.

"Why did you do it, all this time?" Fen asked. "Why help the Rogues? Why act like you cared about them at all? Was that all lies?"

"Not all," they said, fast, panicked. "I wanted... I wanted my own House. I figured if Eluvia was doing something crazy enough, she's out, I'm in. You wouldn't have to be like a bird in a golden cage, Fen. I could have been a Monarch, and you could have been free from your promise."

"I would have gone from a cage to a prison cell," Fen whispered. "A bigger space, but jailed all the same. I love Eluvia, she is my mother in this life, and you are like a sibling. I was in a cage of my own making, all for myself. Who are you to unlock it?"

"Eluvia has never *loved* you," Lorcan spat. "This is something precious about you, but God, sometimes I cannot stand it. You are so blind to her and what she is, even now. You don't see her the way everyone else does, and she likes it that way. You are a pet to her, a very powerful one, always leashed for fear of you wandering too far. And you did just that, with Soren. That is why you need time to think. You need to come to terms with your world and where you stand in it. I could still become a Monarch–"

"Leave."

Lorcan's face twisted in pain, their face pale. "I do everything I do because I *care*, Fen. About myself, yes, but about you, too. Why can't you see? What do I have to do to make you realize I am *right* and that you need someone to guide you? You were never cut out to be a vampire, but you are one, and I am helping you, I'm always helping you–"

"Leave."

"She doesn't *love* you, Fen. God! She is not your Mother, she only keeps you to use you. I'm positive Soren is the same–"

"Leave or I will do something I cannot take back."

"Fen, I–"

"And if you say Soren's name one more time, I will ensure you will not be able to again."

Lorcan's face was red and angry. Their lips parted to speak, but instead they stood, making their way to the door.

"You'll see eventually," they stated, not turning to look at Fen.

"If Eluvia keeps me to use me, then I do not know what to say about your motives, Lorcan. You exist only to serve yourself, and I am just a beloved stuffed toy to you, worn and weathered over time. You want me to be clean and new and exactly in your ideal. You were never my friend, and to you, I was never yours. I am a pawn upon a board, and you cannot stand for me to be on anyone else's side but yours. You are a vampire, Lorcan, through and through. Friendship was not enough. You had to have my power in your own House. But you will find another just as valuable as me, I'm sure."

Lorcan's hand gripped the door handle so tightly that Fen thought it may turn to dust in their hand. They did not speak, and they did not face him.

"Do not come here again," Fen ordered.

As the door opened, a sliver of fluorescent light cutting through the warm glow of the lamp, Fen's thoughts raced so fast he could only keep them within himself for a moment.

Lorcan's right foot crossed into the hall, but the rest of them did not follow.

Fen had shot up out of the bed with a speed he rarely used, his body moving before his mind. His hand yanked Lorcan from behind, causing them to topple to the floor. Fen took their split-second of surprise to slink through the door, slam it shut, and lock it from the outside. He could hear Lorcan's fists pound on the door, their shouts muffled.

Fen did not want to be a pet in a gilded cage or a childhood toy hugged too tightly any longer. He wanted to take walks beside a river and pick up glistening stones. He wanted to go to an art museum and hold Soren's hand tightly as they both pointed at their favorites. He wanted to sit and listen to the rain patter on his window during a storm.

He wanted to be free.

Chapter 20

Soren

Soren awoke screaming.

He was blindfolded and bound, shaking and heaving. A sharp and sudden pain bloomed on his neck and withered in a moment. Then, it was sickening. Blood was being sucked from his neck, pulled from his body with a nauseating squelch from the tube he knew was there. When he attempted to thrash his head about, the speed only increased, and he had to stop to keep himself from vomiting. He wasn't supposed to be awake for this. All the vampires being harvested from were unconscious, blissfully unaware, and he envied them. He wished they had gagged him, to keep him from screaming his throat raw. As it was, his voice would give out before long. Time was not on his mind. He did not count the seconds and minutes; his thoughts were only a whirl of disgust, and there was room for nothing else.

Voices reached his ears, muffled through the wall between him and whoever he knew was watching him from the observation window. He stopped screaming just to hear them, to hear anything but the tubes. He heard the door open and footsteps coming closer to him, and he felt so utterly powerless. There was only one event in his life that was worse than this, but it was dangerously close to becoming a tie.

No one spoke to him. All he heard were echoing footsteps, clinks from objects Soren could not see, gloves being pulled taut, and not one word.

Soren felt a presence approach him, and then the jab of a needle in his arm. He winced, but it was enough to snap his mind into place. Though his arms were bound to his sides, his wrists were not. He blindly reached to grab the vampire injecting him, just barely brushing the fabric of what he assumed to be a lab coat. It was enough. Heat gathered at his fingertips, and he let it loose.

It was refreshing to hear a scream other than his own before his consciousness left him.

-

Soren awoke to nothing but the sounds of the tube.
He smiled when he still smelled a trace of smoke.

The Rogue hoped another Royal would come and make his day, but to his horror, he found that his wrists were now bound as well, and his hands covered by fireproof gloves. His hope changed, instead he wished they would at least come and knock him out again. Anything was better than the sound of his blood being sucked into a vat.

For a while, he rested his voice. Screaming was effective at overwriting his surroundings, but he did not want to cause himself any more pain than what was already being inflicted. As he sat, he heard noises from outside the room again. This time, it sounded like arguing. Soren's ears perked, trying to discern the words. He could not quite make it out, his focus coming and going like a tumultuous tide. But the voices were getting louder.

When the door opened, it was like a bomb went off. A vampire was speaking, rushed, panicked, and afraid. They were talking so fast that Soren could hardly keep up while a second set of footsteps charged into the room, causing a commotion in a cabinet nearby. Bottles fell to the floor and metal trays were pushed aside, all while the mystery vampire was pleading in hushed tones.

"Please, she'll kill me if you do this, I'll do anything you want—"

A yelp of surprise.

"What?! What did you do? I…"

Their voice trailed off and only a *thump* followed.

The other vampire was breathing heavily, unmoving.

Suddenly, Soren felt the presence in front of him and felt the breaths not too far from his face. For a moment, he froze in fear.

At once, the words from the mystery vampire melted Soren away into a puddle of relief.

"It's not fair," Fen whispered, his voice between joking and dismay.

The blindfold on Soren was untied, and he blinked rapidly at the sudden whiteness of the room. His vision came slowly, the blurry image of Fen frantically undoing Soren's restraints nearly enough to make him cry. He would have, if not for the all-encompassing duty he felt. They needed to leave, and fast.

When Fen arrived at the tube upon the Rogue's neck, he faltered. His nail polish was chipped almost to nothing, pale hands shaking.

Soren reached his own hand up and yanked the tube from his neck.

He vomited bile onto the floor immediately, the pain flashing so fiercely that his vision went blank for a moment. Fen was holding him up, and though Soren's body shook, he held him.

Soren wiped his mouth with the back of his hand, resting his eyes upon the vampire lying on the floor. A syringe was sticking out from their upper arm, the contents injected into them.

"Are they–" Soren began, eyes flitting to Fen cautiously.

"No," Fen replied quickly. "Just unconscious. For now. I knocked out pretty much every vampire in here trying to find you. I feel like an expert on this stuff now."

He reached into his pants pocket and held up a bottle full of clear liquid.

Soren was reeling. His whole body felt heavy, his mind would not keep up, and his throat stung. He could not understand how Fen was saving him, when last time they had been in the facility, he was barely able to look at anything, much less use their supplies. There were so many questions, but they did not have the time.

Without a word, they both began to walk out from the room, as fast as Soren's legs could manage.

Fen had been telling the truth. There were several medical vampires strewn about the floors, all unconscious.

"How?" Soren asked.

Fen's face was hard, and his tone was stern. "They can't hurt me, I'm her favorite."

They fled the facility without any setback, Fen carefully easing Soren into the back of a car outside, laying him down.

"You rest, I'll drive."

Soren's body could not argue as fatigue overcame him as the sound of the car engine revved, lulling him to sleep.

-

Soren awoke to a soft touch upon his cheek.

Fen was above him, whispering that he had to wake up, and they were home.

He blinked, wiping sleep from his eyes, painfully sitting up and letting Fen support his body as he exited the car. They were parked at Soren's building, walking into the halls with Fen's arm wrapped around Soren's waist, practically dragging him to his apartment.

Fen swore under his breath, holding Soren tighter. "You need blood," he said. "And probably a lot of it."

Fen fished a key out of his back pocket, unlocking the door and shutting it behind them as they stepped in.

They made their way to the bed where Soren fell onto it graciously, sighing heavily and staring up at the ceiling.

He could hear Fen rifling around in the refrigerator, then felt his touch as he urged Soren to sit up. He did, snatching the carton of blood from Fen's hand and gulping it down. Five cartons later, Soren began to feel significantly better. It felt like he was an injured god, ambrosia now flowing through his veins and making him golden. The sting in his throat eased and the heaviness of his body lifted, though his tiredness did not completely fade.

It was enough to allow him more words.

"How?" he asked Fen.

Fen startled, not expecting Soren to speak. His hair fell wildly around his face, disheveled and stringy with sweat. His clothes were wrinkled and worn, and the polish on his nails had completely vanished.

"They wouldn't hurt me," he said. "I mean that, like, they were ordered not to, and they're too scared of Eluvia to defy her. So I took their shit and used it against them."

Soren was relieved that, at the very least, Fen had not needed to kill. He could not ask that of Fen. That was his job.

"What happened?" Soren pressed, scooting closer so he could rest his hand on Fen's thigh.

Fen bit his lip, his eyes staring down at his feet. "Eluvia… and Lorcan, really, they both… I don't know. I don't know what to say. You were right, Soren. All Royals are evil and horrible and need to die."

"Not all of them," Soren said sternly.

"All of them."

Soren's hand gently grasped Fen's chin, turning his face to meet his eyes. "Not you. Anyone but you."

Fen's eyes welled with tears, and it felt like everything from recent events all crashed over him as Soren watched. "I have to be included," he said, holding back sobs. "Because I still love them. I'm so fucking stupid because *I still love them.* After all that, I can't bring myself to hate them. My sibling, my mother. Twenty-five years as a vampire in that house, and now it's all ruined, and I still can't hate them. I don't want to be near them, but I miss them. I have to be included because only someone who accepts evil would still love them."

"Love could never make you evil," Soren said, watching as tears ran down Fen's face. His beautiful, perfect face, the face of the man who was nothing but goodness. "It is not your fault that they are who they are. It is not your fault that they cared for you. It is not your fault that you could not see, because they hid so well."

Fen did not speak, only cried.

"I wish that love could save them, but it can't, and that is not your fault. They made their choices. You can make your own now, too. I can't claim to understand your love for them, but I understand why the love formed. You will never be at fault."

Soren hugged Fen close, both of them lying down on the bed, clinging to each other. They stayed intertwined until Fen gathered himself enough to speak again, voice shaking.

"And what if my love is not enough to save you?" Fen asked, so quietly that Soren nearly missed it.

His heart lurched. Panic rose within him, the thought that Fen might think Soren would give up his revenge, if only he loved him hard enough. But Fen did not know where it stemmed from, only the thorns that grew from it. Soren had to tell him. His only hope was that after, Fen would accept it, and let Soren light Eluvia ablaze.

"Let me tell you a story," Soren said. "After we've cleaned up. How does that sound?"

Fen inhaled deeply, steadying his breath. When he exhaled, he detached himself from Soren, urging them both up. Hand in hand, they both strode to the bathroom, and Soren only put up a little bit of a fight when Fen demanded to wash him.

"I want to see what they did to you," he said. "So I can work on holding a grudge."

And Soren laughed, the first laugh of the evening. He let himself drift into lighter thoughts before the inevitable storm. He hoped Fen would be able to weather it.

Chapter 21

Soren

Soren, a mortal child of eight years old, ran along a riverbank with three children from the same orphanage. Three boys and one girl, all four of them tossing rocks into the water, watching the ripples form and fade. Cane was small, though he was the oldest, and had a meekness the rest of them did not harbor an ounce of. Sabel was headstrong and loud, the gaps of her missing teeth only making her large smiles all the more charming. Soren was second in command. He was taller and knew what he could get away with in front of the caretakers.

Lysander was above them all.

His blond hair shone in the sun, his athletic nature and quick mind overtaking them all the moment he arrived. He always had the best ideas, the funniest pranks, and the most convincing excuses. Soren thought he might watch Lysander become a king one day.

The ripples eventually bored them, and three pairs of feet ran back to the house before the caretakers would notice.

Soren watched the last of the ripples fade and wondered where they went in such a hurry.

-

At thirteen years old, still mortal, Soren was guided into the most lavish house he could have imagined. A large staircase stretched before him, leading to a second floor he was sure was as grand as the first. He met a boy a year younger than him, dressed in name brands and with a face that would not look at Soren. The hand upon Soren's shoulder belonged to a woman whose beauty blended so effortlessly with the house that Soren thought she may as well be a painting hung on the wall. The man introducing the younger boy was handsome and kind, everything Soren had wanted his Father to be.

The younger boy spent his days in his own company, much to his parents' dismay.

"You wanted a brother," the Mother said to her son one evening while Soren hid behind the wall.

"Yeah, a baby brother. He's older than me, Mom, and he's not even cool. He just writes to his friends all day, he doesn't even do anything. He's boring."

Soren left to go write another letter.

He gave the letter to his Mother, and she smiled sweetly, telling him she would mail it when she went out.

Soren and the younger boy fought for the first and last time that same day. He had been sitting out in the yard, holding a rock up to the sun, marveling at its lovely green color. He thought maybe it would be his new favorite, and then the younger boy stepped in front of him.

"Dad says we need to play," he said bitterly. "What're you doing?"

Soren shrugged, closing his hand around the rock. "Nothing."

A wicked glint shone in the boy's eyes, and Soren knew the look well from his time at the orphanage.

"Let me see," he demanded, holding out his hand.

"Will you give it back?" Soren asked.

"Yes, whatever, just hand it over."

Soren obliged, watching as the boy threw the rock as far away as he could, into the pond farther up the yard.

"Fuck you." Soren said it without thinking, as the venom in his voice he had been keeping at bay reared its head. He immediately regretted it.

The glint in the boy's eyes sharpened before he sprinted into the house.

Soren stayed in the yard, watching the ripples from the rock dissipate. He hoped that the pretty green rock would not hate its new life at the bottom of the pond, so far from the sun.

The boy was back, face red from running. A cardboard box was in his hands one moment, then toppled onto the ground the next. The contents spilled out onto the grass in front of Soren.

"Mom told me not to tell you when I found these, but this is payback. So don't ever be mean to me again." Every word fell onto Soren's ears as if they were being said underwater.

Every letter he had written was on the ground, his sloppy handwriting on every envelope, but one.

Soren picked it up, pulled out a piece of paper, and realized it had already been opened. The letter was from the orphanage, and his mind spun faster and faster with each word.

Dead, it said. All three of them. A tragic accident. The river washed them away—a true shame—right after being adopted. They told the children not to play by the river, but they never did listen. Cane, Sabel, Lysander.

Soren never wanted to watch the ripples again.

-

Soren, twenty-five years old and still mortal, knocked on the door of an apartment with fading numbers and scratched paint. His knuckles were white as he gripped the letter in his hand, crumpling the paper. It had to be true. He did not know what he would do if it weren't.

When the door opened, he smiled for the first time in what felt like years.

"Soren!" Lysander said, blond hair in a buzz cut, with the same face Soren had known.

Without a second thought, he embraced Lysander tightly, trying to keep tears from falling. The other man hugged him back, laughing happily.

"You're alive," Soren whispered, pulling himself away. "What about Cane? Sabel?"

"All here," he said, gesturing for Soren to enter the apartment. "We're… roommates, I guess that's a word you could use."

"What happened?"

For just a moment, so small Soren must have imagined it, Lysander had that glint in his eyes Soren knew. But Lysander had never had it before, so he shook it off.

The door shut and locked behind them, and Soren noticed there was hardly anything in the apartment. No personal items, just furniture that all looked like it came with the place.

Before Soren could walk into the living room, Lysander stopped him, stepping in front to block him.

"Now, Soren," he began, tone playful. "What you're about to see… you need to keep an open mind. Whatever questions you might have, I'll answer them, just promise me something."

"What?"

"Don't run away."

When they entered the room, Soren did not believe what was in front of him. He couldn't. None of it was real, he knew that. There was no way.

Sabel was there, and her smile showed an emotion between mischief and hunger. Cane was there, too, though his mouth was gagged and his eyes screamed for help. He was bound to a chair, and though he was an adult now, his frame was still far more frail than that of the others.

Soren's mouth was so dry he feared he would never be able to speak again.

"So… say hi!" Lysander urged, patting Soren on the back.

"Hi Soren," Sabel cooed, leaning a hand on the chair that Cane sat in.

"Now, you have options here," Lysander began. "Totally up to you. Either Sabel turns you first, and then you can join us in the game, or she turns you after the game, and you get to watch and see how it's done."

None of the words he was saying made any sense to Soren. Nothing made sense.

Sabel sighed. "You're not going to explain any of that to him? His brain might explode before I can turn him."

Lysander ran a hand along the back of his neck, thinking.

"Fair enough," he conceded. "Soren, here's the condensed version. We were all adopted by a vampire King. His house is awesome, by the way, you'll love it. He decided to make the best House, he had to hand-pick the people in it from the get-go. So, in came us three. He faked our deaths to make sure no one came asking about us, and had us all turned when we became adults because can you imagine child vampires? Nasty. Anyways, here I am with a Blessing that'd really impress you, I mean it. Sabel has the Blessing that can turn others, super handy. But Cane..."

Lysander trailed off, shaking his head.

"Well, Cane got nothing. Not even a lame Blessing, he got literally *nothing*. Even when we were kids, he wasn't all that cool, but that really just sealed the deal. So, what do you do with a vampire that has no Blessing? Our King told us that's a no-no, which Cane knew, by the way. This is all par for the course."

"Lysander," Sabel snapped. "Wrap it up. I'm getting impatient."

He gave Soren a *can-you-believe-her* look, and shrugged.

"Fine, okay, whatever you say. So then, I told the King I knew this other kid from the orphanage. I told him this guy, Soren, he's something special, always has been. We can find him, have him join the house, and now we have a Cane replacement! That also means we get the gang back together."

He pointed to Cane with his thumb. "Well, ignore that guy. The gang that actually matters is back together!"

"So which will it be?" Sabel asked, taking a few steps towards Soren. "Vampire now, or vampire later?"

Soren could not speak; he could only move. He lunged toward Cane, reaching for the gag on his mouth, and succeeded in pulling it down before Sabel restrained him.

"Fuck, please let me talk to the King, we can all be together! I'll do anything you guys want, I'll be a butler for all I

211

care, or just let me go! I can be a Rogue! You'll never see me again, I swear on my life."

Lysander tsked and placed a hand upon Cane's shoulder. Cane's eyes went wide, mouth agape, and then he was silent.

"Using my Blessing on him feels like a waste," he said, turning his face to Soren. "But how else do I get him to shut up? He never did learn that particular skill. So, with my Blessing, I'm showing him an image in his mind that'll make him piss himself."

Sabel, holding both of Soren's arms back, chuckled into his neck.

"Can I?" She asked Lysander.

He sighed. "I was hoping you'd be a little more chill about this, but you'll have nothing but time to get over it. We'll just have to share Cane with you, which I don't mind, because you're still my best friend."

Sabel's fangs plunged into Soren's neck, and the pain was searing. His body was on fire and it burned so badly he thought it might kill him. He watched as Lysander pulled a dagger from his ankle and cut across Cane's neck in one swift motion. He dipped his head down, and began drinking while Cane sputtered blood from his mouth.

"Shit, I forgot," Lysander said. "Not enough to kill him."

212

The dagger pierced his heart, and then he was motionless.

Soren toppled to the ground, wheezing and holding a hand to his neck where Sabel's mouth had been. The pain was over, and his body felt incredible.

Sabel yanked him to his feet, leading him to Cane's neck which was still pouring red, and he felt like an animal being led to water.

"Drink up," she said, gently pushing his head down.

He cried into the blood, salt mixing with iron in his mouth.

"It takes a bit to get used to," Lysander said, patting Soren on the shoulder. "But the King will have you up to speed in no time. Being a Royal is the best, you're going to love it. We're rich and we can get away with just about anything. The King is part of the Delegation too. They're like vampire politicians, they make and enforce all the rules, which means *we* make the rules. We have a room ready for you at the mansion, so don't worry about anything."

"Unless he isn't Blessed," Sabel said icily.

Lysander snapped his fingers. "You're right! Hey, Soren, feel any power tingles?"

Soren felt them in his bones. Underneath his skin was lava instead of flesh, molten and itching to be set free.

"What's the King's name?" Soren asked, his voice hard and brimming with fire.

"King Cecil," Lysander answered. "Now, how about that Blessing?"

"Where does he live?"

"Dude," Lysander whined. "Blessing, then we get to all the boring stuff."

"Fine."

Sabel ignited first, her screams shrill as they filled the apartment. The fire alarms went off, obnoxious beeps mixing with agony.

"Wow!" Lysander exclaimed, taking a step back. "I knew you would have a good one, I told them! Wish you didn't set Sabel on fire, but I'm fine with it just being you and me."

Soren reached his hand out, flames burning so hot between his fingers they flickered blue at the center. His breathing was ragged and frantic as his feet slid across the floor to reach Lysander.

The Prince's eyes became wild, fear and adrenaline clear in his face. "Me? Really, Soren, killing *me*? You have nobody else! We're good enough to rule this whole city if we wanted, and we could be brothers *forever.* No one could separate us, not even time."

"I have a family," Soren rasped, taking another step.

"Yeah, me. The people who adopted you aren't your family, no matter how nice Mommy and Daddy were. I am all you have. I made sure."

Soren stopped moving, though the flames still raged.

"What do you mean?" Soren seethed.

"Go to the house and find out," Lysander challenged. "I'll show you, we can go together."

Soren's voice was quiet and so full of malice. If he spoke it aloud, would it become the truth? Could he hold off on what he already knew? Despite his fear, he spoke.

"What did you do?"

Lysander's smile was so vile that Soren could no longer stand the sight of him. He did not care if he would be alone.

Lysander burned like all the rest that would come after.

-

At twenty-five years old, turned mere hours ago, Soren looked at the same grand staircase he had seen countless times before. He had not been back to visit in some time, having been too busy with school and work, but he told his Mother and Father he would make it to dinner as soon as he was able. Even if his brother were there, he wouldn't miss it. That he hadn't made it until now was simply another regret to weigh on his mind.

The blood on the stairs had pooled at the bottom, rivers of it still flowing down from the top. Mother was halfway down, her limbs sprawled in different directions, all in the wrong ways. Father was at the bottom, his face resting open-eyed on the floor, drowning in crimson. His brother was at the top of the stairs, and Soren only knew it was him by what was left of the body.

Soren walked out to the pond in the backyard. It was the same as it had always been. He stepped into it, walking into the water as he submerged himself. When he dove down, his eyes saw in the murky depths better than he had anticipated. He searched and searched, never needing a moment to surface. He may as well have been there for days. His search did not stop until he held that green stone in his hand, and he held it up to the moon as he broke the surface of the water. Though the sun would no longer see its beauty, the moon would have to suffice.

He had no other choice now.

Chapter 22

Fen

Looking out onto the city, Fen listened to the serenity of night and turned a mossy green stone over in his hand. Soren had shown it to him, saying, "It reminds me of you, now that I look at it again." Fen did not know what to think. He had never likened his eyes to anything so lovely, never thought they were worthy of such praise. Soren seemed to disagree, and who was Fen to deny him? He was finding the task of denying Soren anything quite impossible, and it felt as though it was sitting just under his skin, prodding. If Fen asked for what he truly wanted, would Soren give it? Could Fen survive if the answer was no?

Fen's arms were beginning to ache, the metal of the balcony railing digging into his skin for too long. He stood straight, shaking his body out to wake himself up from his daze. The sun would rise soon, and it would be time to sleep. He could hear the clatter of dishware and running water through the balcony door that he had left open just a crack. The two vampires had shared a quiet dinner, Soren lost in his thoughts as Fen had tried to reckon with his own.

He understood Soren's hatred, but it was finally clear to him what was so different between them. Soren had been faced with evil, and he had killed it. He was a man who slayed the demons that came too close, while Fen would hold them, though they hurt him just the same. Fen wished he had that kind of strength, but at the same time wished Soren never needed to know it himself.

The balcony door slid open slowly, and Fen turned to face Soren.

His hair was nearly dry from a shower, and an oversized t-shirt nearly reached the bottom of the black boxers he wore. The sight of him sent a shiver down Fen's spine. This was for him, this barely contained fire made flesh, dazed and sleepy. He found himself wanting to hold as tight as he could to whatever life they could have together.

"Isn't it too cold out here?" Soren asked, tone casual, though a bit nervous.

Fen shook his head, his mouth too dry to speak.

Soren's brows knitted in concern as he stepped towards Fen, making his way behind him. He hugged him tightly and rested his chin on Fen's shoulder.

"What's on your mind?" he asked.

Fen was glad that he could not see Soren's face. He could not bear to see him as he spoke, anxiety seizing all his nerves. They would not have a future if he did not ask.

"Will you stop?" Fen said, letting the words rest for a moment. "Would you ever give up this life? The one you have is full of burning bodies and hatred and I just... you need something better, kinder. You deserve a kinder life."

Soren's body went rigid, his breaths slow and calculating. He did not speak for a full minute, only the sounds of the city below keeping them company.

"No," Soren answered, and Fen's heart felt as if it had been torn out of his chest, leaving nothing at all.

"The Royals who wronged you are *dead*, Soren. You killed them. Why was that not enough? I know you're still hurt, but we..." He stopped to correct himself. "You, I mean. You could be done and you could live happily. You don't need to be a hero. You don't need to be a martyr."

Fen attempted to pull Soren's arms from his body, but he only held him tighter. It sparked a sadness so deep inside him that he thought he may wither.

"The ones who hurt you are still alive."

Fen froze. No, no, no.

"You may not forgive me, but it has to be done. I fear that more than death, but it cannot stop me."

Not his Lorcan, not his Eluvia, not his family.

"I want that kinder future, but I will not have it without you, and without seeing Eluvia dead. I refuse."

His home was already burned to the ground. Would Soren burn all of what he had left?

"I hate seeing you hurt, but I cannot let her go, Fen. I am not the only one they took blood from, and it will only get worse if they continue. They will make the Sun Potions, and they will rule everything, and more Rogues will die. She is the key, and I need to make sure she never opens that door."

He knew it was true, but why Soren? They could run away together and be done with it all, let the rest of the Rogues handle it. His love did not need to be the one to save them all—he only needed to save himself.

A million thoughts raced through Fen's mind. Could he forgive Soren if he did this?

He did not want to ask the question on his tongue, but his resolve to hold back had worn to the bone.

"For me?" he asked. "Would you give it up for me?"

He turned himself to face Soren, hands shaking.

"Would you do it for us?"

And Soren kissed him.

It was hungry and it was desperate and it was impossible to break from. Fen gripped the back of Soren's shirt fiercely, pushing him against the railing. He would be swept away, he was sure. His mind was already beginning to cloud, his body melting and wanting.

Soren was the one to break away, breathing shallowly and resting his forehead on Fen's shoulder.

"I'm sorry," he whispered.

Fen laughed, the sound breaking some of the tension between them. "Use your words, stupid."

Soren sighed, lifting his head to meet Fen's gaze. "I have to do it," he said, his face pained and vulnerable. "But after... I think maybe after she's dead. After I've done it, I could give kindness a try."

Was that enough for Fen? He was not sure, and did not think he would know the answer until it was all said and done. All he knew at that moment was that he wanted at least one more night before his life was well and truly uprooted. Just one night without thinking about death and Royals and betrayal. He needed it.

"I can't say if that will be enough," Fen said carefully. "Not yet. I need more time, just one night at least. Is that okay?"

Soren nodded. "One more night."

Fen held Soren's hand, and began to lead him inside, sliding the balcony door closed behind them. The space between them closed as well, Soren shedding his shirt as they stumbled to the bed clumsily, laughing all the while. Fen ran his hands along the Rogue's body, and then switched to using his lips. He kissed along his hips, his stomach, his chest, their bodies warm against the shuffling sheets. Soren's hands were in Fen's hair as he sighed blissfully, eyes half-lidded and lips parted.

When Fen's mouth came to Soren's neck, he stopped. There were still traces of healing there, the memory of the tube and the facility causing a strange feeling within him. He knew the feeling may be ugly, but he could not help it.

Soren noticed the pause, and tipped Fen's face up with a finger upon his chin.

"What is it?"

"It's not fair," said Fen, echoing his words from when he had found Soren.

"What's not fair?"

"That they had your blood before me."

Soren became voracious in an instant, his hands tugging at Fen's hair as his mouth opened for him.

"Take it," he whispered, the words nearly being swallowed. "I am yours for as long as you'll have me. All of me."

Fen had never had another vampire's blood before. There had never been anyone so special to him, never anyone he felt so strongly for. He felt his fangs sharpen, and he gently ran them along Soren's body as he felt the man shiver. If only once, he needed to taste him.

His fangs sank into Soren's neck, and he felt blood slowly pool upon his tongue. It was like no other blood he had before. It was as if madness and need had become a taste, as if pleasure was a thing he could drink. Nothing had ever driven him truly crazy, but this could become an addiction. Death and forgiveness were not on his mind, nothing but Soren, Soren, Soren. His body, his voice, his very soul, all were before him all at once and it was mania. He licked the wounds, blood smearing on pale skin, and the sight alone was almost enough to send him over the edge. There was never going to be a day he did not crave this again.

Without saying a word, Fen let the feelings carry him, Soren just barely able to keep up. They were a tangle of bodies and nothing else. Everything was dissolving before him, until he snapped himself into reason, but for a moment.

223

"Me too," he urged breathlessly, positioning himself so that he would be on his back, Soren straddling him.

Soren gulped as Fen turned his chin up, showing his throat clearly. "Are you sure?" he asked.

Fen ran his hand down Soren's chest, stopping just above his boxers. "I'd be upset if you didn't."

Soren's smile down at him was enough to make up for a lifetime without the sun. If there were ever a way to have that kind of future together, the moon would be more than enough for him.

Chapter 23

Soren

His love, hair of the night sky and eyes of a forest awash in blissful lust. He could not look away from the face that had saved his life in ways he knew not how to verbalize. If he held it, would Fen realize just how breathless he made him? Time passing and deeds done only furthered what Soren could describe as insanity. He had never felt this way before and knew he would not again. A thousand years and a thousand more rebirths could pass and he would still taste his skin, his blood sweet on his tongue forevermore. This is what obsession meant, he realized it then and there. The depths of his desire would never find an end, he knew it to be true even if death closed its hands over his throat again and again. There was not a way on Earth's soil that he could explain it to Fen, he could not find the words. He never would. It all flashed, red and white and so hot that his mind felt nothing else. He hoped that if Fen did not feel the same, at the very least he felt a fraction, as that would be enough.

He pulled Fen close and kissed him with a hunger that could not be brought to heel. He kissed back, and Soren's body shuddered with the overwhelming sense of sustenance; this was his food now, this passion and this flesh. Fen's fingers curled, nails biting into Soren's skin, and it made him go mad. His last remaining thread of self-control had snapped upon tasting Fen's blood, and it was joyous. A symphony of two bodies played, like an intricate violin performance just for them. It was fast, their hands the bow and their bodies the instrument. They both played as though the music were the only thing connecting them to life. It was desperate as much as it was patient, hungry as much as it was full.

If this was to be his last night with Fen, even his last night alive, it would have been worth it.

-

Once the sun had set, the two vampires had woken, arms and legs tangled together as they rubbed sleep from their eyes and spoke to each other softly. Soren got up to make coffee, and Fen wrapped a blanket around himself and made his way to the balcony. Soren snuck a glance at his back before the blanket had a chance to cover him. Fen caught him, and rolled his eyes with a smile before sliding the door open and stepping into the night air.

It had to be the night Eluvia died. Lorcan would be a nice bonus, too, if he could manage. He did not need to tell Fen; things were teetering on the edge already without him breaking the balance before he needed to. They could pretend awhile longer; they could love each other awhile longer.

As he finished stirring in some sugar and creamer for Fen's mug of coffee, he heard muffled yelling from the balcony. Without a second thought, he raced to the door, relieved when Fen was there, though less so when he turned to him with a heartbreaking look on his face.

"Lorcan is here," he said, his body trembling. "They want to talk."

"I don't give a fuck what they want," Soren spat.

"I know," Fen said, and Soren could see gears turning in his head. "But... I think I want to."

"What?" Soren asked incredulously.

"I think I need closure. At least, that's what I want."

"The closure," Soren began, venom lacing in his tone. "Is that they are evil, and shouldn't even get the privilege to look at you, let alone speak to you again."

"I know," Fen said again. "But I need to do it. In case you… in case I never see them again."

Soren felt guilt pull at his stomach, a harsh ache sitting within him. He would be the reason for Fen's hurt, for Fen's loss. He told himself it was for the best. It had to be.

"You can come with me," Fen offered, eyes testing. "It's probably not a great idea to go alone anyway. Just let me talk to them down in the lobby. You can supervise, and then they leave, and I come back up here to drink the coffee you so lovingly made for me."

As if I would've let you go alone in the first place, Soren thought. He knew he had to tread lightly on the topic of Lorcan for now, and if the closure would make Fen happy, he would deal with it. Besides, Soren did not want to risk burning down his own apartment.

"Fine," Soren sighed. "Let's get dressed."

-

Lorcan stood there in the lobby, hands in the pockets of their annoyingly bright suit pants, staring out the window. When Soren and Fen walked in, they turned their gaze to Fen with a careful smile and a small wave, though when they saw Soren, their expression turned icy.

"Did you have to bring your pet volcano?" they asked, gesturing to Soren.

Soren opened his mouth to retort, but Fen beat him to it. "He goes where I go. You can say what you have to say in front of him."

Lorcan sighed, pinching the bridge of their nose. "It really would be much easier for everyone involved if you had come on your own. I suppose we can just add it to the list of things you'll need to get over at some point."

Before the two men could respond, Soren heard a shift behind him, and turned to stand face-to-face with the real Lorcan as the double's speech faded. They lunged forward and jabbed a syringe into his arm, though not before Soren's hands erupted into flames, Lorcan jumping back just in time to miss the worst of it. He had flung his hands to Lorcan's face, the fire still managing to burn half of it, and Lorcan cried out in pain, holding their own hands to the burns.

Soren was slowly falling unconscious, his body unable to hold himself up, thudding to the floor. Lorcan was swearing, though they used a shaking hand to reach for another syringe.

"It'll at least be painless for him. You're welcome, by the way. Eluvia wanted to keep him for harvesting." They were speaking to Fen, uncapping the needle. "A silver injection would usually hurt like hell, but because he'll be asleep, he won't feel it. Again, you're welcome."

Soren looked to Fen with slowly blinking eyes, and he thought maybe he was dreaming. This whole time it was a dream. They were still in bed, sleeping soundly, the sweet taste of Fen still on his tongue.

The Fen before him was holding a silver dagger to his own chest, his hands gripping it so tight that he thought he may drop it to the floor. It was the one Soren had given him on the mission to the facility, his own personal weapon that had been safely tucked into one of his drawers. Fen must have taken it while Soren had been getting ready in the bathroom. The image of Fen's messy bed hair was strangely the only thought he could solidly focus on.

"If you kill him, I won't be coming with you alive," Fen said, eyes hard-set directly at Lorcan's burned face.

Soren could not stay awake long enough to hear their answer.

Chapter 24

Fen

Fen wanted to hate; he wanted to feel vitriol and disgust and be someone who could thread hands with violence. It was as if savagery were in sight, but he was looking through a magnifying glass, thinking it was bigger and closer, close enough to taste. In reality, it was miles away, and he knew it would never draw near. Though Lorcan was next to him, staring out the car window and watching buildings go by, Fen could only taste sadness. He had made Lorcan swear on their own life that Soren would not be killed. He was sure they knew he was bluffing, but they had agreed nonetheless. The Prince pictured his Rogue being hauled like a ragdoll into another car, his unconscious form being transported to the facility they had just managed to flee from. It would have killed Fen to see Soren die again, and he wondered for a moment if that was selfish. Would it have been kinder to let Lorcan kill him? It was too late now.

The drive seemed to stretch on infinitely, yet at the same time felt as if only seconds had passed, his confrontation with Eluvia coming too soon, yet not soon enough. He supposed the

231

inevitable birdcage would be there regardless. Captivity at the hands of the woman he loved as a Mother may not have bothered him as much, but now dread was keeping him company. When the car finally stopped in front of the oppressive facility, Lorcan exited in a huff. They walked over to Fen's side and opened the door for him, and Fen felt a nauseating pang of guilt. He should not have felt guilty for the slowly healing burns on their face; it was what they deserved. Fen's heart did not share the same sentiment.

"Get out," Lorcan said gruffly.

Fen complied. He was a trained bird, clipped wings and all.

As they strode towards the door, Fen looked around to see if another car was coming, perhaps one carrying his fire. A large vampire, donning a black suit and sunglasses despite the nighttime, yanked his arm, causing Fen's body to jolt in surprise. The man did not speak, but Fen got the message and picked up his pace.

As they entered, Fen let his eyes unfocus, his feet following Lorcan seemingly on their own. He did not want to be present here, not again. So, he let his surroundings drown around him, his mind swimming in its own pool, away from the ocean of horror he was already far too deep in. He let himself submerge in thoughts of red; so much red, the loveliest color he had come to know. A streak of it in hair, a flash of it wrapping around pale skin, the vision of it on a neck and the taste of it on his tongue. Bliss would be a commodity for him now, so he treasured the color and all the comfort it would hold for him. Memories would have to be enough for the bird he was now, flightless as his life had become.

Lorcan entered a room that Fen did not bother to pay attention to until the burly vampire pushed him inside and shut the door behind him. It was an office, the layout eerily similar to Eluvia's study in the castle, though the feeling inside was sterile rather than warm. A desk sat in the middle of the room, two harsh-lined chairs on one side with one much more plush version on the opposite side. A pristine laptop was just being pushed aside by a lovely tan hand as the door slammed shut, and Fen would know the hand anywhere.

"I brought him," Lorcan said, trying their best to keep their tone even. "May I leave?"

Fen watched as Eluvia took in the sight of Lorcan's burned face, and a small smile adorned her deep red lips. "I see the troublesome one certainly kept his tune."

"He's still alive," Lorcan spat, the topic of Soren seeming to crack their composure. "This one threatened his own life, so you see my dilemma here."

When Eluvia turned her gaze to Fen, he suddenly felt so small, like a child being chastised for breaking a dish.

"And he is being escorted here?" She asked her question to Fen, her eye contact never wavering even as his own flitted about the room.

"I don't know," Fen said.

"Good," she answered, dismissing Lorcan with a wave of her hand.

They left, though not before giving Fen one of the most bitter looks he had ever seen, and whispering, "You should have let me kill him. He is in for a fate far worse, and that's thanks to you."

The thought hurt him more than Lorcan's words, but he knew it was true.

The door opened and closed heavily, and then it was just Eluvia and Fen.

She gestured for him to sit, and he did not move.

Her brows creased in annoyance. "Sit," she said, and so he did.

They sat in silence together for what felt like an hour, Eluvia's nails tapping on the desk rhythmically, her eyes never leaving Fen. It was more and more suffocating by the minute, a magnetic feeling pulling at his mind.

"It is harder now," Eluvia said, finally breaking the silence. "That boy cast his influence on you far better than I gave him credit for."

Fen did not say anything. He feared he would cry if he did.

"My language has many words I could use for him," Eluvia began, nails still tapping. "Though the words I could have used for you have changed, my dear. No longer are you free to roam as you please. In time, you may earn this again. As it is now, you will stay here while the castle is rebuilt. You will not leave. You will speak only to me. You will be here in the event that I require you."

Fen nodded, a lump in his throat getting more painful every moment. He would agree to it all, but he had to be brave. For Soren.

"What about Soren?" he asked, voice barely a whisper.

"You will not see him again. He will live, on that you have my word, as I understand that if he dies, so do you. Whether he forgives you for that or not, I cannot promise."

He will never see Soren again. His love will live a life he never wanted, and he will wish himself dead, and he will hate Fen.

"In time, I will choose someone suitable for you. If you keep yourself well, you will be rewarded. If not, loneliness will become your companion."

Eluvia's face twisted, her smile becoming so spiteful and devious that Fen could not look away. He missed who he thought she had been.

"*Eres mío*," she said, and Fen's whole body felt as if it had been compressed, the air forcefully being pushed from his lungs. "You are mine."

He felt the words in his bones, and his eyes began to well with tears. All of Fen's logic screamed that she was never to be loved by him again, that she had forfeited it the moment he had learned the truth. His affection told a different story, a story of a woman who had saved him at his lowest, who had given him a home and a family. Hatred felt closer than it ever had, brushing his fingers, just out of reach. He needed to grasp it, to hold it and let it overtake him.

But when he looked into Eluvia's deep brown eyes, so full of disdain, he still could not hate her.

He realized that hatred could be achievable, just not for Eluvia or Lorcan. Fen's hands wrapped around it, the feeling overwhelming him to the point of physical pain in his chest. Hatred of himself was the only form he would know.

As Eluvia's gaze dug holes into Fen, a sudden shake of the door handle rang out into the otherwise silent room.

The door opened in a rush, slamming into the wall. Eluvia's eyes tore away from Fen, and his breath became much more abundant without her scrutiny. He took a panicked breath as he turned his head to face the commotion.

It was Lorcan, their face wild and their hands shaking. Their fear was so strong that Fen felt part of it himself, terror bleeding into him.

That's when Fen smelled smoke.

As the scent hit him, the world slowed so much that Fen thought maybe time had stopped completely. He watched as Lorcan went to shut themselves in the room, their words high-pitched and strained.

"He's–" was as far as they got before their clothes caught fire.

They screamed and screamed, and Fen watched them crumple to the ground. They writhed in agony, still attempting to crawl into the room as they burned. A hand shot down to their ankle, pulling them out into the hallway, leaving them with whoever else was burning in the hall. The door slammed shut, and there stood Soren.

Fen could not breathe. All he could do was look at a bloody and battered Soren. He had a cut on his forehead that had spilled blood all down his face, and his amber eyes were feral. He looked like a god of war, stained with the carnage of his victories. His right hand was enveloped in fire, and his left was only halfway attached to his arm.

Soren's chest heaved as he lifted his uninjured arm and pointed at Eluvia, fingers forming a gun, the tips so hot they turned blue at the center of the flames.

"You're next."

Chapter 25

Soren

His emerald, his forest, his pretty green stone turning in his fingers in the moonlight. Fen, Fen, Fen. He saw him there, eyes wet and hands shaking, and Soren would kill Eluvia. She would die by his hand, here, now.

I'll kill her, I'll kill her, I'll kill her.

He took a step forward as Fen inhaled and reached for him. Soren wanted to touch him, to feel him again, but first he had to kill her. Fen continued to reach for him, and Soren's eyes met with his.

Lovely, breathtaking, perfect. He would do this for him. He had to.

Just as Fen's hands nearly gripped Soren's bloodied shirt, Eluvia's voice rang out like a bell, clear and agonizingly loud.

"STOP."

Soren froze, and so did Fen.

"I have had *enough*," Eluvia said, standing from her chair and slamming her hands down on her desk. "Fen, look at me."

Fen's eyes had been looking only at Soren, but at Eluvia's words, his gaze went from concern to pain. He was trying to resist her, but Soren knew better. Fen was so full of love and light, and he would not trade it for anything. He gave Fen a small smile and a quick nod, trying to tell him it was okay.

Fen's head began to turn towards Eluvia, but he gritted his teeth and stopped halfway through, trying to turn back to Soren.

Eluvia cursed, hands hitting the desk again. "Fen. Look. At. Me."

Soren watched her face then. Her forehead was shiny with sweat, and her nails dug into the desk. He had to wear her out, let her tire enough to loosen her grip so he could lunge for her.

When face to face with Soren's fire, Lorcan had readily spilled about Eluvia's Blessing. Coercion is what they had said. The more someone knew her, the more trust and affection they had for her, the more power she held over them. It was the same with fear. She would speak, and people would listen. That is why he knew Fen stood no chance.

240

Soren nodded to Fen again, and this time he could not defy her. Fen's face turned to Eluvia, and she smiled.

"Good," she purred. "Now stay in your seat."

The Queen made her way to Soren, not an ounce of fear showing on her dewy face, though Soren's right hand was still ablaze. She looked into his eyes and commanded him over and over not to move, and while he heard the words, he still urged his body to move. She would tire the more he fought back, and so he did.

Soren felt confident until her hand went to his belt, reaching behind his back to find a silver dagger he had stolen from a dead guard. She took it with a triumphant look directly at him, and in an instant, his fire was extinguished, the heat replaced by an all-encompassing pain.

The dagger cut through the remaining connection of flesh between his left hand and the rest of his arm, and blood trickled to the ground. Soren's hand followed, blood beginning to cover it at his feet.

"Shall I do the other?" She asked Fen, and Soren watched as something in the room changed.

The pain in his arm was immense, but his senses focused on Fen, blurring his agony. His love's face was blank, wiped clean of any fear, panic, or concern. Eluvia didn't seem to notice at first, not until Fen stood up.

Eluvia didn't seem to notice at first, not until Fen stood up and spoke. "You won't stop, will you?" He asked, tone matter of fact, accepting.

"Stop what, my darling?"

"You will hurt me forever, I think. That's something I could live with."

Fen's divine emerald eyes turned to Soren, and it made him breathless.

"But I can't let Soren hurt in my place. You will not do that to him."

Eluvia laughed, twirling the dagger in her hand, looking from Soren to Fen, and back again. "I would not waste the energy, my sweet. If you must be kept under constant supervision, it shall be done. But this one," she pointed the dagger at Soren's chest, the tip of it just brushing his shirt. "He is not worth the trouble. The best thing to do to a fire you do not want to spread is to smother it."

Fen's eyes became so forlorn that Soren's own began to well with tears. It was more painful than where his hand used to be, more painful than the cut above his brow, and certainly more painful than anything Eluvia would do to him.

242

Fen closed the space between him and Eluvia, and he wrapped his arms around her in an embrace. She accepted it, patting his back and whispering comforts.

And Fen's voice was so quiet, a whisper coming out of his throat as if the words never wanted to be uttered.

"I am so, so sorry," Fen said this under his breath, and Soren could not decipher if it was meant for him, though dread pulled at his stomach.

Fen broke their embrace, and Soren watched as Eluvia raised the dagger to Soren again, the tip of it just over his heart.

"You will miss him for a time, but all will heal."

And Soren watched his Fen, his Prince, his love. His hands reached for the dagger, so quickly he nearly missed it. His shaking hands took it from Eluvia's grasp, her body turning towards him in shock. The bloody silver of the dagger disappeared into the Queen's chest, all the way to the hilt. Her knees gave way, and Fen released the dagger, instead moving to help her to the ground.

As her eyes began to dim, she spoke. "You wretched boy. You promised."

Fen nodded, running a hand through her hair. "I have to break it. Even if it means another dead Mother."

Soren watched as her life slid away from her body, Fen holding her in his arms. He buried his head into her shoulder, a cry of pure, unfiltered pain erupting from his throat. Soren lowered himself down, wrapping an arm around Fen's shoulders.

And Soren let him cry.

-

The walk out of the facility was filled with smoke and bodies, Fen's cries ringing out into the halls in a song of sadness that Soren could not stop. His love's face was buried into Soren's back as they walked, refusing to look at any more death. They walked out into the night, stealing a car that was parked outside. They exchanged no words as Fen fell into the passenger's seat, head resting on the window, Soren trying to do everything with only one hand as best as he could. That was going to take some getting used to.

When they arrived at Soren's apartment building, all of the injuries and exhaustion were beginning to take a toll. He had to hurry before he collapsed. Soren needed blood, and a lot of it. The wound on his forehead was closing and healing, but the missing hand was a larger issue. It was no longer pouring blood, but the wound would take time to close and heal over.

Soren stepped out of the car, and opened Fen's side, too. He emerged in a daze, holding onto the back of Soren's shirt like a child trying not to get lost in a crowd. Soren's body hurt, of course, but most of all, his heart was aching for Fen in a way he did not know was possible. He would do anything to make him feel better, and a terrifying thought came to his mind. What if he would never be better?

He banished it from his mind. It was not the time to dwell on such things, with his vision getting hazier and hazier with each step.

By the time they reached his door, Soren was spent. His hand could not grip the key in his pocket, the shaking of it too much to control. Instead, Fen took the key, unlocked the door, and led him inside.

He made Soren sit down at the dining table so he would be upright, and made his way to the refrigerator. Fen swore under his breath, hauling five cartons of blood to the table and setting them down while worrying at his bottom lip with his teeth.

"That's all we have here," Fen said, opening a carton and handing it to Soren.

Soren could not stop the shaking enough to hold it steady.

When Fen saw his difficulty, he smiled softly, trying to comfort him. "I'll help," he said, holding the carton to Soren's lips.

And so Soren drank every carton dry as Fen held them. When they were all empty, he made his way to the bathroom, returning with the first-aid kit.

Fen carefully cleaned and wrapped Soren's arm. The bleeding all but stopped, thanks to the blood he drank. While his body was working to heal the physical, his mind was still a storm of worry.

"What about you?" Soren asked, tipping his head toward the empty cartons. "I only had those, and neither of us are in much shape to go out and get more."

Fen shook his head, his smile hollow. "Don't worry about me right now."

"I always worry about you."

His green eyes bore into Soren with such intensity he thought his heart might stop.

"Let me take care of you," he pleaded. "I need to."

Soren reached out, his hand resting on the back of Fen's neck, pulling him up towards his neck. "Drink," he said.

"You're just getting better," Fen retorted. "That won't help you at all."

"We can take care of each other," Soren replied tenderly. "Please."

Fen's lips brushed Soren's so softly it felt like air, his mossy eyes just inches from Soren's.

"Okay," Fen whispered. "Thank you."

As Fen's fangs sank into Soren's neck, it was a wholly different feeling from before. This time, it was tentative, careful. It did not hurt, far from it. The feeling was like being greeted upon waking, like a rainy day nestled on the couch, like holding Fen's hand and feeling him squeeze back. Comfort covered him like a blanket, and he sighed in contentment.

After Fen was done, they both made their way to the bathroom. He wrapped Soren's left arm in plastic to ensure the wound did not get wet in the shower, and Soren just watched him work. They showered, and the blood that had begun to crust onto them washed down the drain. Soren imagined his hatred like that. He hoped it was washing away just the same.

When they were done and dried, they went to bed as the sun rose outside. Before falling asleep, Soren thought of the words he would say when night fell. He would tell Fen that he was ready. That kinder life was all he wanted; he no longer needed to be the hero, to cause fires and kill. He had seen what that life wrought, and watching Fen kill Eluvia had been the final straw. Never again would Fen have to participate in violence; Soren would make sure of that.

They would be free.

They would be happy.

They would be kinder, together.

Chapter 26

Fen

Fen's eyes fluttered open, his sleep roused by the bathroom door softly closing. He reached over to his side, feeling the empty spot beside him. Before he took his hand back, the quiet tinkling of a bell rose up to the bed, and a wet nose pressed against his fingers. Smiling, his hand rose to greet the silky fur of a rather insistent tabby cat, her purring growing louder with his touch. Fen lifted her, then rested her body on top of his chest. She curled up close to his chin, settling as he petted her gently. The door opened and shut again, footsteps light as they neared the bed. A breathy laugh reached Fen's ears, and it was like bliss had a sound.

"I leave for one minute, and Emmy already stole you away," Soren said, keeping his voice low as he sank back into his spot.

Fen switched hands, using his left to pet Emmy instead as his right went to Soren's forearm, remembering to keep his grip above where Soren's hand used to be. "Why can't you share?" he teased, stroking Soren's skin with his thumb.

"If it's Emmy I'm sharing with, I suppose I could."

"Were you looking again?" Fen asked after a pause had grown between them.

Soren stayed silent, his body turning slightly stiff.

After the deaths of Lorcan and Eluvia, it had taken weeks for Fen to begin life anew. Soren was to thank for it, in more ways than one. Taking care of Soren had kept him going well enough, but nightmares were frequent, and his life felt emptier the longer reality sat with him. The nightmares still came, but with time and Soren there for him, they came less. The move had been the biggest help overall—a new city, a new apartment, a new life. Fen and Soren could explore it all together, the freshness of it all easing the pain little by little. Adopting a cat had been Fen's long-standing desire, and Soren had delivered one evening after all their moving boxes had yet to be unpacked.

Soren had been out procuring more blood cartons as Fen stayed home, curled up on the couch and trying not to drift into a fitful sleep. When Soren arrived home, his surprise had spoiled itself as the cat meowed in protest of being in a carrier. Fen could hardly contain himself, jumping up from his seat and nearly tackling Soren to retrieve the animal from him.

"Let me see!" Fen had said, the joy in his voice making Soren smile broadly.

"Alright, alright! Let me set her down here."

When Fen opened the carrier, a brown and white tabby sauntered out, wholly unfazed by them and the new space. She made herself at home on the couch where Fen had been sitting, and it took all his self-control not to shower her with affection then and there.

"Do you have a name picked out?" Soren asked, wrapping a hand around Fen's waist as they stood to stare at their new roommate.

Fen shook his head, beaming up at Soren. "You pick."

He smiled, and kissed him softly, pulling Fen's body closer. "I did have an idea…"

"Tell me, don't keep me in suspense!"

Soren chuckled as he brushed his lips on Fen's forehead. "Emerald."

Fen buried his face in Soren's chest, hugging him close and inhaling his scent. He smelled of coffee and pine, and Fen thought he may just lose himself in it.

Fen's grip on Soren's arm squeezed lightly, urging him. "Feeling up to talking about it?" Fen asked.

Soren sighed, turning to lie on his side, his left arm stretched before him and his eyes resting there. "I just get these phantom feelings that wake me up sometimes. I have to go to the mirror to check, like I can't believe my own eyes, like my reflection is more trustworthy."

Fen nodded, watching Soren intently. "Can I help in any way?"

"You already do," he replied, moving to cuddle up next to Fen. "Just stay with me."

"I always will."

-

The apartment was dark, save for the TV casting colorful images onto Fen and Soren's faces, their bodies threaded with each other under a blanket, Emmy on the other end of the couch. Time moved on, and it brought Fen great solace. Nightmares still came, and Soren still went to the mirror alone sometimes, but life went on. They would wake with the night, and walk hand-in-hand down the streets of a city they were getting to know more and more. They would try new cafes, Fen daring to try anything while Soren could only brave a select few drinks. Emmy would rub at their legs for food far too early, and they would trip over her and laugh. Fen and Soren would kiss, they would hold each other, and they would sit in comfortable silence. Life moved onward, and it got easier.

While Soren clicked the remote to prompt the next episode, his phone on the side table lit up with a text. Fen grabbed it for him and watched as Soren's face became complicated, his expression shifting with every word he read. Anger, confusion, anxiety, and even relief all had a place.

"What is it?"

Wordlessly, Soren handed the phone to Fen, urging him to read the words on the screen.

It was an update from the Rogues.

When all was said and done, Soren had decided on a simple life with Fen. He would no longer let his hatred drive him like a tempest towards his own destruction. It wasn't his job to save the world, not when he had someone to live for. The Rogues hadn't been thrilled that their best fighter was leaving, but what could they have done to stop him? Fen knew the fire within him was only tepid, and with enough kindling, it could be ignited again. The Rogues knew it, too, and had reached out to him many times in the following months, pleading with him to rejoin. When Soren stopped answering, they eventually stopped trying. Now, after several months, they were trying again.

Though the text had clouded Soren's face, the message held good news.

Without Eluvia's empire, the Sun Potion production had been thrown into disarray, letting the Rogues topple it entirely. While that threat had been quelled, the matter of the Delegation had not yet been dealt with. They would simply appoint a new Royal in her place, and a new scheme would inevitably surface. However, the text stated that the Rogues had taken every opportunity granted to them, in the chaos of everything, to find most of the Delegation members.. At that point, it had been a matter of mutual understanding. Rogue numbers were growing, their ranks far outnumbering the small Delegation, and it was seen as a threat. Either they could work together to make life better for everyone, or it would be an execution. Some of the Delegation attempted to fight back, only to be swiftly disposed of by the Rogues. They did not make idle threats, and they wanted the Royals to know.

So, a fragile peace was in the works. Rogues filled spots on the Delegation, working on ways of governing that would root out as much evil as possible. Things would be better, and they wanted Soren to be a part of that. They wanted him on the Delegation.

A question hung in the air between them as Fen looked up from the phone, his eyes resting on Soren.

Fen did not want him to take them up on the offer, not when they had just found so much happiness in a new beginning. He could not stand to go back to that city and see the remains of his home, everything a reminder that his family would not be coming and of the hurt that they caused. He could not live in the wake of their storm.

But he knew Soren. He knew the offer would tempt him, that the idea of being someone with the power to create change was a thrilling idea. But the position would get him killed, Fen knew it in his heart. He could not stand for his ruby to become someone of blood and fire again. Fen also knew, though, that it was not his choice. No matter how badly he hoped, he knew Soren could go back, that being the martyr would sound too good to refuse.

They sat in silence for a long time, Fen's hands shaking in his lap, covering the phone below them. He did not want to ask, did not want the question to become real on his tongue.

Gently, so gently, Soren reached for the phone. Fen did not want to let it go, but his shaking hands would not heed his desire.

Soren took it, opened the text, and stared at the screen for a moment. He bit his lower lip, brows furrowed, and began to type only one word.

No.

Then he deleted the text, blocked the number, and set the phone down on the side table.

Fen did not know what else to do but cry.

His tears fell as Soren pulled him close, hugging his body tightly. Soren stroked his hair, shushing him softly. "Please don't cry," he pleaded, his voice dripping with honey and warmth.

Relief had flooded Fen so completely it felt like the only emotion he had ever known. He gripped Soren's body as if it might fade away, and he kissed his lips as if they might never be before him again. His Soren. He was there, and he was staying.

After his tears lessened, Fen rested his forehead against Soren's, closing his eyes and taking deep breaths. "You're staying?" he asked, just to make sure it was not a dream.

Soren smiled at him, one that was so sure and solid it made Fen's heart leap.

Emmy chose that moment to stretch, and begin her ritual of begging for food, her meows pitiful.

They both laughed, the tension melting away to nothing and being replaced by comfort instead.

"We'd better feed the little princess before she takes drastic action," Soren said, standing up while lifting Fen with him. "And by that, I mean biting at my heels."

They laughed again, and Fen felt whole. Soren peeled open a can of cat food while Fen pet Emmy to placate her wrath, though she darted away in a flash once her bowl hit the ground.

Soren and Fen stood together then, arms around each other's waists, watching Emmy eat her food happily.

"Do you think we should get her a sister?" Fen tested, turning big pleading eyes to Soren.

He just kissed him in response, the pressure of his lips firm and sure.

"The answer is maybe," Soren replied after they separated.

Fen pouted playfully, but then he rested his head on Soren's shoulder, closing his eyes. Even if nightmares plagued him for the rest of his second life, he knew Soren would be there when he woke. His family did not need to be anything but the man beside him and the cat at his feet. *Well, hopefully two cats,* Fen thought.

"You'll stay." Fen said it not as a question, but as a statement with a voice full of hope.

He felt Soren turn his body to face him, and they looked into each other's eyes.

Soren, with his messy brown hair, the streak of green turned white instead, "To match Emmy," Fen had said, as it was his idea. Soren, with his amber eyes bright and focused only on him. Soren, with his life now his to do with what he wished, freed from the shackles of his hatred.

Fen didn't know if he would ever be free from his own memories and thoughts, but he now knew his freedom came in a different form. He was no longer a bird in a gilded cage. He was settled down in a tree of his choosing, longing only for the life of kindness that stretched before him.

"I always will," Soren said.

His Soren, forever.

The End

From the author:

Thank you so much for reading my debut novel, "With a Cast of the Dice."

I had set out to write what I want to read: queer romantasy that features adult characters, but isn't too far from YA. Fen and Soren became so dear to me as characters the more I wrote, and I knew I wanted a happy ending for them, even if they had to traverse some fires along the way.

Huge thanks to my editor, for loving these vampires as much as I do, and to my boyfriend, the one who let me ping-pong ideas at him while I furiously wrote the plotline at the library.

I plan to write many more queer stories, and I hope you'll come along for the ride.

Magnus October

www.ingramcontent.com/pod-product-compliance
Lightning Source LLC
Chambersburg PA
CBHW020556180626
46810CB00007B/2529